KNIGH
MIRR

Garthe approached. H
thousand tightly-stru
post whose structural integrity was less than a sure bet. His words spat forth like bullets from a gun. 'Let me introduce you to reality, as a victor,' he snarled. 'I am about to defeat you, and, like the villains in the spy movies I so dearly adore, I'm entitled to a speech, and the speech is this: I am going to crush you, and your pathetic Foundation for Law and Government . . . And I will squash Michael Knight like a cockroach . . . As rightful heir to the Knight name, I will destroy FLAG. You. Her. Michael Knight. And when the smoke clears, the only thing that will remain will be me.'

Also available in Target:

KNIGHT RIDER
KNIGHT RIDER II: TRUST DOESN'T RUST
KNIGHT RIDER III: HEARTS OF STONE
KNIGHT RIDER IV: THE 24-CARAT ASSASSIN

KNIGHT RIDER V
MIRROR IMAGE

Glen A. Larson and Roger Hill

Based on the Universal Television Series
'Knight Rider'
Created by Glen A. Larson

A TARGET BOOK
published by
the Paperback Division of
W.H. ALLEN & Co. PLC

A Target Book
Published in 1985
by the Paperback Division of
W.H. Allen & Co. PLC
44 Hill Street, London W1X 8LB

Printed and bound in Great Britain by
Anchor Brendon Ltd, Tiptree, Essex

ISBN 0 426 19932 4

For
ANDREW SNIDERMAN
a fellow Fleming scholar

1

It was a hundred and ten degrees outside.

Michael Knight disinterestedly checked the temperature readout and was silently thankful for the state-of-the-art air conditioning unit – perhaps the most mundane component of the car he was driving, but one he was thankful for nevertheless.

The drive from Los Angeles to Las Vegas took about four hours, and Highway Fifteen was more or less a dead straight line connecting the City of the Angels with the gambling capital of the West. It was mostly Mojave Desert flatland between the two, featureless desert scrub and level road from which milky waves of heat shimmer pulsed. The only distraction on this trip was a wretched little oasis called Barstow, a refuge for rednecks and shotgun-toting provincials, that sat steamingly hot and shadeless, in the middle of the trip. Michael preferred to breeze right through it. Were he piloting a normal car, his only available diversion would have been music tapes or the radio. Or whistling.

But Michael was not driving a normal car.

'*Michael, I suppose you know we're in violation of the law again*,' the car told him, with a faint tone of snide irritation.

His eyes watched the erratic red grid-screen mounted above the steering column. It was called the vox-box, and provided a visual display to accompany the patterns of the car's speech. The voice seemed to be that of a prim colonial tutor, with a patrician Boston twang to the vowels.

'What are we doing wrong now?' Michael said, anxious for any diversion.

'*We're exceeding the posted speed limits, which specify fifty-five miles per hour.*'

'Only by fifteen miles,' Michael sighed. 'We're barely crawling.' He knew from recent experience that the vehicle he was driving was capable of surface speeds in excess of 250 miles per hour. 'You mean you want to slow down and enjoy Boredom City for maybe another hour?'

The car did not answer; it often clammed up when it was miffed.

Michael was speaking to the microprocessor locus housed within the impenetrable, molecularly-bonded, black armour hide of the Knight Industries Two Thousand. Acronym: KITT. Status: Partner to Michael Knight – a partner that had saved his hide on numerous occasions from several kinds of skinning. The sleek black automobile combined all the technological advances created by the multibillion-dollar Knight Industries cartel into a single mobile, intelligent unit. As an all-inclusive information centre, urban tank and highspeed companion, it lacked only one element – a driver of complementary capacities.

Knight Industries had discovered that man in Michael Knight, formerly Lieutenant Michael Arthur Long of Homicide, Reno, Nevada Police. Left for dead in the desert following a high-stakes sting operation gone awry, Lt. Long was saved from death by Wilton Knight, the Howard Hughes of Knight Industries, who had descended from the sky like some mythological being to spawn progeny from his own forehead.

And indeed, thought Michael now, as he drove KITT along the flat desert highway, he *had* sprung fullblown from Wilton Knight's head. The ancient corporate wizard had handed his dying body over to a team of surgeons who had reconstructed his face – a face obliterated by a point-blank pistol slug that had rebounded from a metal plate in his forehead – and when the bandages had come off, Lt. Long existed no longer. In his place was the spitting image of a younger Wilton Knight. Michael had promised Knight on his deathbed that he would attempt to realize the old man's buck-the-system dreams, and after Knight's funeral discovered that he had become Michael Knight – surrogate son, the vehicle for old Wilton's unfulfilled philanthropic wishes, with all of Knight Industries at his disposal.

Devon Miles, a dour British gentleman and Wilton Knight's able right hand man, had detailed Wilton's proposed FLAG program – short for Foundation for Law and Government – to Michael. The pilot program was to put in the field an independent, troubleshooting unit, a balance of man and machine. Michael was a headstrong maverick, perfect in crunch situations thanks to his police experiences and his undercover work in Viet Nam. He could think on his feet, and KITT could supply whatever resources he lacked.

There were doubts, and arguments, and objections, but there had also been fate. Michael Knight sprang fullblown into the world, to assist those who could not assist themselves, and in a year and a half had run KITT and himself ragged, and confronted near death at least three dozen times.

He stared at his face in the rearview mirror – *his* face now, not Michael Long's, or Wilton Knight's, but his own countenance. KITT shifted smoothly into the AUTO CRUISE mode while Michael's thoughts were elsewhere – two coloured indicators on the control column of the car's Super Dash lit up, and the car drove itself.

Michael's abilities had been sorely taxed by FLAG thus far, but he had more than risen to the challenge – the sheer danger of his new calling had become like a narcotic. He loved taking extravagant risks and living life fully. The benefits were obvious – a unique career, KITT as a partner (and indeed, to Michael the car was an indispensable male chum, not merely a souped-up calculator), and the unlimited influence and resources of the Knight Industries combine. But the deficits had become clear in the ensuing eighteen months of nonstop action – the addiction to danger, with its need for increasing dosages; bouts of exhaustion, during which he paid the physical price for his excoriating lifestyle; a chaotic and unfulfilling love live, which seemed destined to never stabilize; the loneliness of playing Lone Ranger for real.

There was Devon, of course, but he was more a father-figure and guiding hand than an equal. There was KITT, who was not human, and despite the fact that Michael viewed KITT's one-of-a-kind personality as human, there were human capacities the microprocessor could simply never provide. In fact, Michael was often thrust into the role of teacher, instructing KITT on human foibles. KITT's maintenance technician, and the fourth quarter of the FLAG team, was April Curtis, who despite her unparalleled technical ability and superior intelligence, had three big strikes against her – one, she was female; two, attractive; three, Devon's daughter, and strictly off-limits, to Michael at least, for any kind of extracurricular interaction. Her merely being a gorgeous woman would not have caused Michael any problem, but he had recently become aware of the fact that, at least where women were involved, his personal life had been somewhat mismanaged, and the fault was entirely his own. He generally shrugged it off as a consequence of his peculiar calling. Sometimes, alone at night, he worried about it, but he never shared this worry with anyone – anyone human, that is.

The benefits outweighed the hazards. There was one other pitfall Michael refused to consider – *could* not consider, given his personality, and Wilton Knight had cunningly taken this capacity into account when considering Michael's dossier for the FLAG pilot program. The pitfall was that, sooner or later, Michael would not elude death so easily. As years wore on, his reflexes would slow, his adversaries would strengthen, the psychological stresses would overwhelm him, or KITT would no longer be able to fill gaps, or show up just in the nick of time, as in a cliffhanger serial. Michael did not think about this in terms of his job eventually killing him – he did not fear death since he had already 'died' twice – but he assumed he would eventually become like Devon Miles, which meant that one day, inevitably, he would be grooming his own replacement.

Michael's first 'death' had come in a Viet Cong interrogation camp, where he had sustained the severe injuries necessitating the metal plate in his skull. The second 'death' had come in the Nevada desert, getting his face blown off. Result: The first death had caused the second death to fail – the face-shattering bullet had bounced off the metal plate. When the true end of Michael's life came, he knew it would come with serenity, not the violence that had plagued his life.

For now, the future was as endless as the highway, and the fact that Michael was heading back towards the Nevada desert where he had been critically wounded eighteen months before now held no evil ghosts to deter him.

His own rangey, tousled good looks confronted him from the oval mirror. Wilton Knight's reconstructive surgery had left his jaw with a harder edge, the eyes more hooded and cynical . . . but when his own personality peeked through with a wry grin or a bad joke, that face lit up, inspiring friends to confidence and enemies to fear.

And it charmed women, don't forget, he thought, smiling to himself now, as if to prove it. We must never forget about charming the women . . .

He looked up, and saw a charming woman.

She lay on her stomach, face turned towards him, designer sunglasses pushed down onto the tip of her nose. She was topless, and her flawless tan was there for the world to marvel over. A cascade of blonde hair obscured her breasts. Her teeth were perfect, gleaming, beyond a moist and inviting mouth. The curvature of the small of her back was thrilling, the trim fitness of her body astonishing, the length of her beautiful legs spellbinding. She was at least fifty feet tall.

RELAX WITH ME AT THE DUNES HOTEL, LAS VEGAS! said the legend above her. Then the massive billboard flashed by to the right of KITT, and was lost behind them.

'*She's not even half-naked,*' said KITT, sounding like a disapproving spinster. '*More like four-fifths naked. I don't know what you see in women like that, Michael.*'

'Hey, pal,' he said, 'You like April don't you?'

'*Miss Curtis is extremely capable. She does things to me that ten other technicians could not accomplish.'*

'I feel the same way,' he said, cracking a smile. 'So you noticed the resemblance.'

'*Resemblance?*'

'Between April and the girl on the billboard.'

Stuffily, KITT replied, '*I wouldn't know, Michael – I always see April with her overall on.*'

'Me too,' Michael said with a trace of regret. Sometimes, having KITT's scanner capacity to X-ray a target might come in handy. 'But I use my imagination.'

'*Devon would not approve of your thinking about his daughter that way.*'

'I know,' he said airily, not concerned.

'*I've also probed all available data banks,*' KITT said, changing the subject, '*and I have not discovered a single redeeming factor about gambling. I find it difficult to imagine an entire city devoted to the purpose.*'

'It's the lure of risk,' said Michael, who knew better than anyone the attractions of danger. 'Like the lure of four-fifths naked ladies. Gambling deals with odds systems. Mathematics. Trot out one of the computer bank's blackjack programs and I'll show you.'

'*I'd rather not.*'

'Come on, we've still got an hour of drive time. Two bucks a hand, what do you say?'

KITT's number two monitor blinked to life, the video screen displaying the digital twenty-one program. Card numerals were shown beneath their suit – spades, hearts, clubs or diamonds – with the face cards designated K for king, Q for queen, and so on. Numbers blurred as the electronic pack was 'shuffled.'

'I'll be the house,' said Michael. 'You be the player.'

'*I believe the word is "sucker",*' returned KITT.

Michael punched a toggle on the Super Dash, and the electronic representation of the deal commenced. Michael got a nine, and a second card face-down, signified by a green video square. In blackjack, the player's job was to base choices on an assumption of what the dealer might have 'in the hole'.

KITT caught a six and a five. '*I want to double down*,' he said.

The strategy of doubling-down consisted of doubling the amount of one's bet in return for a single draw card. Since the object of blackjack was to get your card total closer to twenty-one than the dealer, doubling down on an eleven was ideal – the largest card value you could receive was a ten or a face card equalling ten, so there was no way to exceed twenty-one, to go 'bust'.

'I think I'm being hornswoggled,' said Michael. He hit the button. KITT caught a jack of diamonds. Eleven plus ten equals twenty-one.

'*Pay up*,' said KITT.

'Beginner's luck,' Michael snorted. Now a balance-due figure appeared in the upper right of screen. 'Get your money down or you don't play.'

KITT's ante appeared onscreen – four dollars, twice his previous bet.

'Hey, this is getting expensive,' said Michael. 'You sure you don't want to save some of that back?'

'*Is the house in the habit of advising the player*?'

Michael laughed. Yeah, in Vegas the dealers were all smiles, more than willing to help you lose your money. 'Okay, it's your skin.'

'*I believe Humphrey Bogart would say, "shut up and deal, sweetheart"*.'

When Michael had lost fifty-six dollars, the number two video monitor came on. 'What is it?' he said. 'You want to play two hands at once?'

'*Not a bad idea, Michael. I could make money twice as fast that way. April is calling in from the Foundation office.*'

'Punch her through,' he said, and the screen lit up with April's face in tight closeup, a ringer for the billboard girl. She looked superlative even given the harshness of the video image, and the unflattering lighting.

'Hey, good looking,' she said, and Michael felt something squirm about in his stomach. 'I see KITT's giving you a bath. I designed that blackjack program myself.'

'I begin to feel I'm being had.'

'*Oh, April gets half my winnings*,' said KITT.

'KITT, you're a doll,' she said. 'Devon's got a pit stop for you guys to make in Vegas.'

'And how is dear old dad?' said Michael cavalierly.

Devon's cultured visage appeared on the screen, with a downturned mouth. 'I am not dear, neither am I old, and a little more decorum, Michael, if you please, in front of April.'

'Aye aye, sir.'

Devon cleared his throat, and spoke too loudly for the camera's microphone. 'There's a Caesar's Palace employee named Rita Wilcox working out on the Strip, and I want to get your impressions of her. She came to the Foundation with a rather offbeat tale about her missing brother . . .'

'Will do. Does she know I'm enroute?'

'No. But do me a favour – check her out for me. See how her story resonates when she tells it to you.'

He began to sense Devon was leaving out a key detail, as he often did when dealing with Michael, to keep the young FLAG operative from backing out on a particular assignment. 'What else, Devon?'

Devon maintained a professional cool. 'I'll be able to tell you more after tonight.'

'He's got a date,' said April, poking her head back into camera view.

'Do tell,' Michael said.

'She's *really* pretty, Michael, and stylish, and –'

Devon harrumphed loudly in the background, and April wisely chose not to belabour the information any more. Instead, she told Michael, 'And you got some mail.'

Michael never received mail, so this surprised him. 'Old creditors? I've been drafted?'

'It's an invitation to a wedding,' April said, obviously reading the gilt card just below-frame. 'It's that David Dalton guy, and Joanna St. John – the two you met last month. They're getting hitched.'

It seemed like yesterday that Dalton, a maverick government man not unlike Michael himself, had saved Michael's life during the Eduardo O'Brien case... and Michael had saved the life of his fiancée, Joanna, during an imbroglio encompassing millions of dollars in smuggled Mexican gold, hired assassins, and a raid on a secret Army weapons depot in the California desert not far from his present location on the highway. When David and Joanna had met, it was like introducing oil to vinegar... but they, like Michael, had ignored the powers of fate. So, in a way, their engagement had been a logical outgrowth of the danger they had all shared. The news made Michael happy, and just a bit jealous – Joanna had been attracted to him as well, and had proved herself sharp, resourceful, and graceful under pressure. 'That's terrific; send them a cable and let them know I'll make the wedding come hell or high water,' he responded. 'And April? What are you doing opening and reading my mail?'

She looked flustered for a beat, then shrugged, 'It's addressed "care of" the Foundation, so I took "care of" reading it.'

'Grand. Tell Devon I'll be in Vegas in about ninety minutes, and I'll give him a full report.'

April winked, and signed off. The screen went blank.

'*I'm not giving up this hand just because of the transmission*,' warned KITT.

'Why?' Michael glanced at the screen still displaying the electronic twenty-one hands. He had a face card up – a healthy sign – and a ten in the hole, for a tough-to-beat total of twenty.

'*Because I believe this is a blackjack*,' said KITT. His own hand appeared on the screen – a queen and an ace. '*I win again. Unless you wish to hit your potential twenty, in the hopes of getting an ace*.' In the unlikely event that Michael lucked out and drew one of the three aces remaining in the deck, they would tie, or 'push'. Some casinos let a bet ride on a push. In others, the house claimed pushes as wins. Michael was piqued at his bad luck, but not stupid enough to hit on a twenty. He had known tourists, playing blackjack, who weren't as smart.

'No thanks. I think we'd better wrap this up and go introduce ourselves to Devon's mystery girl.'

'Being a sore loser won't get you your money back.'

'Put it on my tab, old buddy.'

2

Michael and KITT hit the Strip section of Vegas at dusk, just as the billions of wattage in neon signs were firing up for Caesar's, the Aladdin, the MGM Grand, the Sands, the Dunes, Circus Circus, the remodelled Flamingo, the Thunderbird, the Silverbird, the Barbary Coast, the Royal Las Vegas, and all their sister gaming establishments and resorts. The image most people commonly held of Las Vegas was the Strip at night, blazing with tourists, and light, and hookers and slightly sinful fun. Las Vegas in the daytime was much uglier, much closer to the truth. In the daytime you could see the garbage littering the streets, the bums and winos wandering into hotel restaurants for their coupon breakfasts and free rolls of nickels, the traffic accidents clogging up the Strip. At night it was glorious, and the morning after was always too bright, and depressing. At dusk, it at least did not give Michael the headache he expected.

He turned into the parking lot of Caesar's Palace during the height of the dinner hour, so parking was relatively simple.

'Don't go away,' he jokingly advised KITT. 'I'll give a yell on the comlink if anything intriguing scares up.' He pressed the wrist-radio device to broadcast a test-tone. A little graph appeared on the tiny liquid-crystal screen indicating that the comlink was in good working order, with a full battery charge.

'*Don't gamble away the money you owe me*,' KITT returned.

Michael stepped out into the blast-furnace heat of Las Vegas. It is a choking phenomenon like walking face-first into a smelter, rarely mentioned in the tourist brochures. Then, the sliding glass doors of Caesar's sensed his approach, and slid back to receive him. A second set of doors slid open as soon as the first pair closed behind him, and Michael felt why the airlock effect was necessary: The air-conditioning inside the casino made him feel as though he'd jumped out of an industrial steam press . . . and into a meat freezer.

Gambling activity was minimal on the wide promenade of tables; most folks were eating about now, or dressing up to see a show. Somewhere behind him, in the maze of blinking slot machines, a fat woman screamed as 'her' machine belched out a spray of dimes. A man in a cowboy hat, playing Mini-Baccarat, hooted as he collected his winnings in twenty-five-dollar chips. He finally had to scoop them all into his hat.

The table minimum for blackjack at Caesar's had gone up to three dollars several years back; it was hard to find a two-dollar table anywhere on the Strip, and impossible to find a one-dollar game anywhere except on the 'no-armed bandits' – the blackjack machines. Michael had been getting off easy by playing KITT.

All of the bored-looking blackjack dealers in the horseshoe-shaped arrangement of tables wore nametags. Michael scouted around until he found one that said: HI! I'M RITA FROM CARSON CITY. She was holding forth from a table where the minimum bet was ten dollars.

One man sat at first base – the seat immediately to the dealer's left, the first position to receive cards in a left-to-right deal – and he was sweating despite the air conditioning, which must have held the interior temperature at around forty degrees. He laid down a panic bet and gave up his last chip as a tip to the dealer. As he pushed back from the table, cleaned out, his eyes met Michael's.

'Don't play against her if you're thinking about it, friend,' the man said, mopping perspiration from his brow with the sleeve of his cheap suitcoat. 'The good-looking ones are always pure poison.'

'I feel lucky,' Michael countered, sliding onto a stool as the other, more heavyset man shambled away.

Rita's full mouth was open, and there was recognition in her stormy blue eyes. Her close-fitting dealer's blouse and apron revealed just enough for Michael to verify that she was a hale and attractive woman of fulsome dimensions. Her gaze was laser-sharp.

'Garthe?' she said. 'Jeez – did you shave off your moustache? You look so –'

'I hate to say this,' he interrupted, 'But I'm not Garthe, I'm Michael – Michael Knight. The Foundation sent me to –'

He stopped talking when he saw the sexy flush of recognition on Rita's face quickly replaced by the cheesy paleness of sudden fear. She swallowed and fought to find her voice. 'I told them not to send anybody *here*!' she whispered harshly. 'I can't talk here!'

'Then deal,' Michael said easily, laying down a ten-dollar bill in the betting circle.

'Cash plays,' she announced over her shoulder to the pit boss, and shuffled four decks of cards into a dealing shoe. She regained her composure, hiding her surprise.

Michael caught a five and a six – eleven. 'A friend of mine always advised me to double down on eleven,' he said, digging for another ten dollars to cover it.

She flipped him a single card, face down, then turned her own hole card over. She had a total of seventeen, and by the rules at Caesar's, had to stand, or not draw more cards to increase her total, since the chances of busting increased. Sticking the dealer with a seventeen was a nearly ideal situation – there were many combinations that could pay off. Michael turned over his double-down card, and to his horror saw that he had caught the deuce of clubs. The double-down permitted him only one card, and now his total for the hand was an anaemic thirteen. He watched his twenty dollars vanish into the table's cash slot, forever.

'So much for my Mississippi riverboat gambler friend,' he said with a broken little smile.

'I get off at midnight,' said Rita, *sotto voce*. 'Meet me by the fountain, outside, okay?'

To pass the time until midnight, he tooled around greater Las Vegas, bought some magazines, stored away a dinner at a place called the Green Shack, and lost some more money to

KITT at computer blackjack.

She appeared at the appointed location precisely at 12:02, and he escorted her to the car. Like most people who rode in KITT's passenger bucket, she gave the blinking and jumping readouts of the Super Dash a cocked-eye glance of interest and confusion.

'Thanks for the lift,' she said, more at ease now. 'And for waiting. Hated to do that but, you know, they're watching us all the time in there with cameras and stuff, and I don't want them to think I'm cheating the casino.' She crossed her legs in the deep footwell; they were a striking pair of legs, nicely outlined by black hosiery.

'You've been a dealer for a while?'

She fidgeted, then launched into a story she'd obviously told before, many times. 'I came here to be a nightclub singer – with my brother, Ron, you know? He played keyboards and was just a musical wizard with pop-funk.'

Michael stifled his immediate response. Everyone came to Las Vegas to be a star, as if it was some kind of low-rent version of Hollywood. Those women who didn't achieve overnight fame, and didn't become dealers, either became waitresses or prostitutes. Or they hightailed it back home, to whatever dingy small town they'd left behind for fame.

'I saw the light of practical reality,' she continued, 'and decided to go to dealer's school. I was surprised it was so easy. The shifts are bearable and the tips are good. And then, I met this guy, Garthe, the guy I thought was you.'

'The guy you thought *I* was,' Michael corrected.

'Yeah. He was Mister Mysterious. But amazingly nice, in a kind of cold, prepared way. He deluged me with gifts. A bouquet every day to my apartment. Trinkets that cost me a whole week's pay *plus* tips. One of his gifts was a job for Ron – several jobs, actually. Odd little pickup assignments. He never really discussed it, so I suspect it wasn't all above board.'

'Some kind of unspecified criminal activity?'

'*I* thought so. But by then, you know, he was sending a limo to my apartment to pick me up for what he called his "evening outings". More flowers – so many that Ron's allergies started kicking up. I got carte blanche at all the hotel shops . . .' She shook her head and finished with a sad smile of tarnished remembrance.

'But the plot thickened somehow,' Michael prompted her. 'Lavish waste wasn't enough?'

'I *enjoyed* it, I guess,' she said. 'But I've always been a sucker for romance, you know? The screen goes all hazy, the music swells, the lovers embrace, and the camera cuts to waves crashing on the beach. Garthe was brutally pragmatic. He made it clear to me that he prefers to buy whatever he wants, outright.'

'Your view was a gothic romance, and his was a porno novel?'

'Something like that. It left a bad taste in my mouth. So here I am, dealing cards for a living again. So much for my big splurge. But in the meantime, Ron found out something about Garthe – something that made him nervous enough to collect his information on tape, as a safeguard, he said, against getting "erased".'

'Ugly term.'

'I don't think his precautions saved him,' she said with regret and loss. 'I think he got in trouble, and from what I know of Garthe Bishop, he could easily have been killed. But his safeguard is still floating around, and I don't think Garthe knew about it.'

'You have the cassette tapes of what Ron found out?'

She shook her head. 'No, but I've got the key to the locker the tapes are stored in. I have no idea where the devil the locker is – somewhere in Vegas, I suppose, since there's no I.D. on the key. He mentioned stowing his safeguard in a locker and left the key on our key rack, so he wouldn't have it on him.'

'And then he just . . . vanished?'

'Like somebody waved a magic wand,' she nodded. 'This is it. Casa Wilcox.' She pointed at a cinderblock apartment building and Michael pulled over to the kerb.

He could tell from the exterior of the place that it was an inexpensive, no-frills, basic lodging... quite a step down from the level of limousines and daily bouquets. She handed him a bronze locker key, started to close her door after thanking him for the lift, then hesitated.

'Do you know what the word *antithesis* means?'

Michael smiled gamely, at sea. 'That one wasn't on my Word-a-Day vocabulary builder this month.'

'You're the antithesis of Garthe Bishop – the opposite. Garthe without the earring and moustache. You seem benevolent; he's sinister. Like twins. Or Dr Jekyll and Mr Hyde. The resemblance is uncanny. I think I like you, Mr Knight, but please be sure of one thing.'

'What's that?'

'Garthe Bishop isn't going to like you, one bit.' Then she turned and nearly fled to her apartment.

Michael sat there wondering just what on earth Devon had got him into *this* time.

'My dear, darling Devon,' said the woman in the grey silk evening gown. 'Do come in – Jordan, please take Mr Miles' coat, would you?'

Devon Miles stood in the doorway of the tastefully appointed mansion in the Trousdale Estates district of Beverly Hills, having arrived right on time for the appointment April had so frivolously called a 'date' during the transmission to Michael. A balding, effeminate servant sidled up to collect his hat and coat. He reminded Devon of the sort of character Dwight Frye used to play in every Universal Pictures monster movie made before the second World War. Jordan the butler was a bug-eyed, unctuous creature who spend most of his time scuttling forth just when the woman in grey required something.

Elizabeth Bishop, however, was another matter entirely. She stepped forward and collected both of Devon's hands into her own. She had the look and poise of gracefully ageing royalty, living proof that beauty, charm, and a birthday sometime near the middle of Franklin Delano Roosevelt's administration as President were not mutually exclusive.

'You look absolutely wonderful,' she said, hanging onto his hands. 'Mature. Distinguished. Urbane. Quite the ladies' man.'

'It's very good to see you again, Elizabeth,' he said. 'You're as beautiful as I've always remembered you. Neither memory nor fantasy does you true justice.'

'I'm flattered, sir,' she said coyly, without seeming ridiculous. She led him into a parlour lined with walls of bookshelves, a gleaming ebony baby grand piano, and a south wall of glass panes that afforded a breathtaking view of the city at night. Drinks, already prepared, awaited them at the hardwood wet bar. The creepy Jordan had already slithered away.

'I'm impressed,' Devon said honestly. 'I'd always known you held by the maxim, "living well is the best revenge".'

'No one's invented a better phrase. I'll stick by it. Vodka and tonic?' She lifted a glass.

'Ah. You remembered.'

'Of course.' She stared at him eye-to-eye, leaning on one small fist on the bar, watching him, examining him, drinking him in. Devon finally turned his attention back to the window – discreetly.

'I was surprised – though pleased – at your phone call to the Foundation. It's been well over three years.'

'Three years, six months, ten days and . . .' she consulted a diamond-studded watch '. . . twenty hours. But who's counting?'

Devon was surprised by the speed with which his old, accustomed caution around Elizabeth leapt back. He had always been wary of her, and knew that her capable directness and considerable charm could become keen-edged without warning, like a concealed weapon suddenly whipped forth.

Anticipating him, she beat him to the punchline: 'I suppose we've known each other too long and too well to dismiss my call as a social excuse to see you. You're waiting for me to tell you what I want, correct?' Her smile had not wavered.

'Yes.' He decided simplicity and civility were the best courses. Let her do the talking.

'You should know better, Devon. When Sigmund Freud was on his deathbed, the acolytes that gathered around him asked him if there was any question his philosophies hadn't found the answer to.'

'And Freud said, "What women want." There's no need to be cryptic, Elizabeth.'

'There's no need to rush, either. Allow me a moment to savour the past – the Foundation has seen very little of me these past years for reasons we both know too well, and prime among those reasons was my strong attraction to you, even when I was married to Wilton Knight.' Elizabeth had been the elder Knight's fourth wife; the marriage had lasted four years and broken apart several decades previously. A generous Knight stipend, paid biannually, had kept her comfortable, and her investments had been quick to pay off.

Strangely, he was still attracted to her as well. Even more strangely, he was beginning to enjoy this flirtatious fencing.

'The attraction still exists,' she concluded, 'and the future is unaccounted for.'

'The last time we spoke was in 1979,' said Devon. 'What have you done since then?'

She shrugged, a gesture at once imperious and modest. 'Everything the tabloids say a wealthy divorcee does, I suppose. Although I'm sure you wouldn't be shocked by any of it – no one as worldly as you would be.'

He smiled warmly. 'I gave up being shocked years ago.'

That made her laugh, and her laugh made him happy. 'I've had Jordan prepare some hors d'oeuvres. Shall I call him in to serve?'

'As long as he leaves immediately afterward.'

'Excellent,' she nodded. 'I want you all to myself.'

'Sounds ominous. Or perhaps, hopeful. Are you sure you don't have some ulterior motive tucked neatly between the canapes and the small talk?'

She broadcast a sage expression. 'Ah, but *I* gave up ulterior motives years ago. When I desire something from a man, he's generally aware of what I want.'

The temperature in the room seemed to be rising subtly. Devon said, 'Perhaps we can open a window as well, and enjoy the view.'

'That's what servants are for,' she said. 'Let's get Jordan out of the way for the rest of the evening, shall we?'

She yanked on the bellrope with anticipation gleaming in her eyes.

'You'd better not have another twenty,' Michael warned KITT, dourly staring at the blackjack display on the number two monitor. 'That would be three in a row.'

KITT revealed his hand – a jack and a ten. '*Twenty beats nineteen. Thank you, Michael.*'

'Stop thanking me!' he said as he drove back to Caesar's. 'It's just beginner's luck.'

'*Correction. It was beginner's luck yesterday. Today I am no longer a beginner, in addition to which luck is no longer a factor. The odds for blackjack give the house – you – an advantage of point-six percent. But if the player uses logic and –*'

'Okay, okay. Did the analyzer give us anything on the key Rita gave us?'

'*Tests reveal little. The key was ground from commercial stock blanks, available anywhere. Not likely we can trace the locker from the key . . . but I'm working on it.*'

'Ready for another hand?' Michael said it as though his doom was a matter of record.

'*April is calling.*' The other monitor lit up.

'Hey there,' Michael said. Then he looked at the screen.

April looked harried. She also appeared to have stayed up all night, or slept in her clothes. 'Michael? You've got to come back to L.A. right away!'

'What's up?'

'It's Devon – he went on his date last night and –'

'And he hasn't come back yet,' Michael chuckled. 'That sly old silver fox. April, don't worry about him; I'm sure he can take care of himsel –'

'No, no, you don't understand! He's here, right now, in the study with Dr Alpert. He wants you to come back immediately.'

'But I haven't finished with Rita Wilcox yet. He told me to find out about –'

She interrupted him again, upset. 'Michael, Devon was poisoned last night!'

Across the parking lot of Caesar's, Michael saw Rita and several other dealers about to check in to begin their shifts. He had to catch her before she was inside. 'I'll be right back!' he shouted, jumping from the car and jogging across the lot.

Rita turned to intercept him. 'Is it the locker? Did you find out something already?' Hope glistened in her eyes.

'Uhh – not exactly.' His head was still reeling from the news about Devon. He pictured his friend laying in a bed, connected to beeping machines, comatose or worse. 'Rita, I have to raincheck you for a day or two. There's been an accident... er, an emergency at the Foundation. It can't wait.'

Her expression of hope hardened into a gaze of betrayal. 'What you're trying to tell me is that my missing brother just doesn't measure up, in terms of global importance, to your errand, right?' She pushed her shoulders back, as though she had expected such a cop-out.

'No. I'll be right back. I just need a day to –'

Rita had already turned her back on him, thinking he was dissembling. 'I'll have to get what I want some other way,' she said, disappointed.

There was no time to argue. He had to find out what had befallen Devon. He called KITT over via comlink, got into the pilot bucket, and prepared to make tracks for L.A.

He checked the rearview mirror one last time for Rita. She was already inside. But standing at the casino entrance was a man holding a slim black cane, flanked by two mean-looking ebony bodyguards. It was difficult to tell from the shaky reflection, but he looked like Michael . . . with a moustache. Could this be the mysterious Garthe?

Michael couldn't tell, because at that moment his spectral twin disappeared inside the casino.

3

Michael watched Devon bustle about his suite at the Foundation's Los Angeles offices, feeling somewhat guilty about burning up the road to get home when Devon now seemed so spry. He squinted at his mentor, searching for some visible sign of his brush with death, some obvious handicap left over from his bout with the poison April had mentioned over the radiophone.

'Are you *sure* you're okay to travel?' he said.

'Oh, don't be so annoying, Michael,' Devon said, too quickly. He was shaken up, but wouldn't show it, and under his agitation there was a scary kind of fear Michael had not seen too often in his eyes – he had been rudely surprised as a result of his 'date'. He steadied himself against his desk, then glanced at Michael and April, defying them to notice. 'Dr Alpert assures me I'm in excellent condition . . . right now.' He looked beaten and defensive. 'Or words to that effect.'

'Devon, *talk* to me, blast it all,' demanded Michael. 'What's going on?'

Devon leaned against the desk, something his usually military posture rarely allowed. 'Boiled down, this is what it seems to mean: Wilton Knight's son, Garthe, has somehow resurrected himself from a death sentence in Africa – the Jimbaru Province. Getting out of that place alive is something akin to escaping Hades without singeing your eyebrows. Impossible. But he managed it.'

Michael concealed his surprise by using anger. 'I knew there was something you didn't bother to tell me regarding the Rita Wilcox assignment. I had no idea it involved a son of Wilton Knight – especially since you led me to believe he *had* no offspring.' His pique grew as he recalled Wilton Knight's deathbed scene, the occasion where the elder Knight had impressed upon Michael the importance of carrying on the honour of the Knight line. That all seemed to be so much bad dialogue now.

'Michael – he was going to tell you,' said April in her father's defence. 'We didn't expect events to turn quite the way they did ...'

'Oh, great. So you knew, too? As usual, good old Michael's the only one in the dark!'

'Michael, shut up!' Devon snapped. Recovery from the toxin he had been dosed with had eroded his manners and patience. 'I'll explain if you'll hold yourself in check for two minutes ... unless even *that* simple feat is beyond you!' Devon's eyes were bloodshot, his skin clammy, his hands slightly quivering. Michael wisely decided to back off; Devon enraged, even under normal circumstances, was a spectacle that made him feel petty and stupid.

'I'll fetch us all some coffee, okay?' April said, fostering a truce.

'I'm listening,' said Michael, arms folded tightly.

'Elizabeth was Wilton Knight's fourth wife. They were divorced many years ago, but she did bear him a son.'

'Garthe?'

'Yes.'

'Don't tell me – black sheep of the family, and all that, right? Alienated from his father early? At cross purposes with Wilton's career plans for him? Am I warm?'

'Garthe left for Europe when he was seventeen and never returned to the States. For a period of years, despite all of Wilton Knight's resources, the only available intelligence on Garthe said he'd become involved with revolutionaries and terrorists – the Black September people, the Red Claw Tongs, supplying armaments to the Mau Mau in Africa. This last got him into a spot of trouble in Jimbaru.'

'The death sentence?'

'A Tongo M'Kimbe death camp in the heart of Jimbaru Province, at the height of the suppression of the revolution there.'

'I'm surprised he wasn't skinned right away.'

'While he was awaiting execution, he was befriended by Tsombe Kuna. You know the name?'

Michael nodded. 'The main man of the so-called Pan-African Liberation Movement – the terrorists who use the little palm tree as their insignia.'

'Tsombe Kuna was freed by a PALM raid; he took Garthe out with him . . . that is, we *think* that's what happened.' Devon spread his arms to indicate the enormity of what they did not know. Speculation had to fill in the gaps – even news correspondents found out nothing in the war-torn province . . . except how to get their own hides out of the country during the thick of a revolution. 'Garthe had extorted a great deal of deeded African land in the southern part of the country. Much of the property incorporated diamond mines that had been shut down for being unsafe.'

'Sounds like Garthe and Tsombe Kuna made a deal.'

'Garthe supplied the real estate, and Kuna provided the labour force. His Red Berets are fanatically devoted, crack troops. They would follow any order Kuna gave, no matter how outrageous.'

'And he ordered them to take up diamond mining, to re-establish a financial power base.' Michael understood.

'They needed high-technology weapons in order to make themselves a viable threat. But more than that, Kuna and Garthe became fast friends, based on a mutually parasitic relationship. During their first year of operation, they pulled approximately fifty million dollars out of their illegal diamond mines.'

'That's quite a cash base.' April had returned with the coffee tray. Michael served himself while she tended to Devon.

'I'm convinced,' Devon continued, 'that Garthe contacted his mother sometime last year. Whatever they're planning together has been in the works for at least that long.'

'What about the, um . . .' Michael stroked his shaven chin.

'... the family resemblance.'

'Partially the fault of genes,' said Devon. 'Garthe was the spitting image of his father. Partially Wilton himself – you see, he never quite got over the loss of Garthe, particularly when Garthe ran so contrary to everything Wilton believed in. It was easy to imagine his son dead. And so, when the doctors were surgically rebuilding your ruined face, their reference came not only from the old OSS photographs of the younger Wilton, but from the very few photos that existed of Garthe. Wilton didn't even keep them in the house; he never looked at them, or mentioned Garthe's name. But the use of the taboo Garthe photos was by explicit order of Wilton's.'

'You were the guy who pulled the photos,' Michael recalled.

'Yes, and to me, at the time, it wasn't a deception. Garthe Knight was dead for all of us. And Wilton had to exploit what he saw not only as an opportunity to launch his FLAG program... but to "remake" his lost son, literally in his own image, as you accused him of doing when you first came to us. I was offended by your cheek, then. Now, I acknowledge it as a bitter truth.'

'So Wilton Knight got what he wanted all along – the FLAG program, piloted by a "good" version of his errant son.' Michael whistled slowly between his teeth. 'What a spectacular foul-up...'

'Only because Garthe didn't die in Africa, as he was probably destined to.'

Michael shook his head. 'Destined to? You mean because he was "evil"? You know, Devon, a lot of the African people hold residual superstitious beliefs. Maybe Garthe survived through the power of his own evil. Maybe he's a zombie, returned to haunt Wilton Knight... only he's a bit too late.'

'That gives me the willies,' said April.

'I don't believe in the supernatural,' said Devon, with rock-hard conviction.

'He goes by the name of Bishop, now, according to Rita,' said Michael. 'What about that?'

'His mother's maiden name – the one she received her support cheques from the Foundation under, as I recall,' said Devon. 'Ironic, in a way.'

'How so?'

'Chess values,' said April, catching on. 'In chess, pieces are assigned point values. A queen is a nine, and a pawn is a one. If you can trade a queen for a pawn, you're eight points ahead. The knight and the bishop, in chess, rate three points each – they're equally matched.'

He stared at the pretty blonde incredulously. 'Well, I suppose if you hadn't brought up that little bit of trivia, KITT would have.'

'I haven't finished his new, improved chess program yet,' she said.

'Don't bother. The blackjack program is murdering me as it is.' He turned back to Devon. 'Okay, so Garthe and his mother are reunited. He's got enough money to buy anything he wants – at least, what Rita told me at Caesar's verifies that he's rolling in cash. And when I spotted him outside the casino, he had two very humourless black goons flanking him.'

'Out-of-uniform members of Tsombe Kuna's elite guard, the Chiruwis – the word is derived from the African denoting a kind of vicious tribe member, an expert on medicinal knowledge, who only shares that knowledge if wrestled to the ground. They rarely speak, even to each other. The only thing they enjoy is fighting.'

'Terrific,' Michael said. 'So with all these resources, what could Garthe gain by having his mother take advantage of an old attraction, and invite you over to slip you some poison that didn't work?'

Now Devon appeared positively uncomfortable. 'Although it didn't kill me, Michael, I'm afraid the drug might have achieved its purpose.'

'What are you talking about?'

'You asked what Garthe wanted. I think he's after the chemical formula for the Bonded Molecular Shell.'

'The stuff that makes KITT's skin impenetrable,' clarified April. 'The secret ingredient that's kept you alive and breathing through all those missions.'

'Wilton Knight foresaw the danger of recording the formula anywhere. Instead, the components were divided into three groups of two each. Each two-ingredient list was entrusted to a hand-picked confidant. Wilton knew the entire formula of course, but hypnotized himself in order to lock it up in his brain behind certain key words none of us knew. However, the three aides were his fail-safe. Any two of the three could combine their knowledge and reproduce the formula – but one, working alone, could not.'

'You talk as though you were one of the three.'

'I was. That's what has me concerned.'

'I ran a data fetch on the other two men,' said April. 'Prof. Henry LaCosta is alive and well in Geneva. But Dr Kyle Elliot disappeared from his hotel in Rio de Janiero last Tuesday . . . and no one has seen him since.'

Devon picked it up. 'Dr Alpert identified the toxin residue in my blood as an extract from the African gum tree. It's called *oluta.* Masai warriors used to tip their spears with it. In more sparing doses, *oluta* serves quite nicely as an herbal version of sodium pentathol – truth serum.'

'Elizabeth Bishop slipped you an *oluta* mickey?'

'Right into my vodka-and-tonic. I was so suffused with self-satisfaction at seeing her again I never noticed the flat taste. Five minutes later, *bang*! Darkness. And I woke up with April and Dr Alpert hovering over me.'

'That's when I called you in Vegas,' April said.

'Okay,' Michael said, trying to extrapolate. 'Assume Garthe and his mother, in cahoots, got the formula components from Devon's head, and are working on Dr Elliot. What do they do with the Bonded Molecular Shell once they've got it?'

'Garthe gives it to his good friend, Tsombe Kuna,' said April. Gradually the implications sank in around the room. 'And together they armour their tanks and vehicles with it, even stick it on fibreglass body armour . . . and Kuna's Red Berets overrun the continent of Africa. Garthe's personal fortune in diamonds increases maybe a thousandfold, considering the land they'd take over. I've seen computer projections on Kuna's land-based assault forces. When I factored in the Bonded Molecular Shell, the odds of even such a small strike-capacity army taking over the continent one country at a time jumped alarmingly.'

'It would be like having a fleet of cars like KITT, with weapons, to utilize blitzkrieg-style. Kuna's idols are Idi Amin and Hitler . . . but he draws his tactics from Rommel and Patton. He could do it.'

'Devon, let me go back to Vegas,' said Michael, eagerly. 'Rita's brother Ron *had* something on Garthe – a satchel full of cassette tapes, stashed in a locker somewhere. KITT and I didn't have time to find it. But maybe it'll give us a lead on Garthe.'

'Elizabeth cleared out of her Beverly Hills house,' noted April. 'She's long gone.'

'I *saw* Garthe in Vegas. Whatever he's up to, he needs to be in Vegas for some reason!'

Devon considered this, and nodded. 'April, do you feel up to a quick trip to Rio de Janiero?'

'Will I have any time to sit in the sun and get rid of my tan lines?' she asked, not hopeful of an affirmative response.

'Absolutely not,' affirmed Devon.

'Let's go, then,' she said.

Michael keyed his comlink open. 'KITT, have you monitored and recorded all this data?'

'*Affirmative, Michael,*' came the car's report. '*All tucked away in the memory cells.*'

'Good. Then I'll bid you guys a quick *au revoir*. Let's find out just how good Garthe and Elizabeth Bishop really are – just how many points they're really worth, right, April?'

She smiled in response, and for no particular reason Michael thought of the girl on the billboard, in the middle of the Mojave desert.

4

'Michael, I've never had the Garthe Knight/Garthe Bishop data in my memory banks,' protested KITT. *'This is as much news to me as it is to you. I've never even met this Garthe, and I must say that I much prefer your company to what I've learned of him.'*

Together they streaked back towards Vegas on the burning highway.

'Rita was right, it seems, when she mentioned Dr Jekyll and Mr Hyde,' mused Michael.

'It must have been a trial for Wilton Knight, to have such a son. Wilton Knight embraced intellect, reverence for the individual, and not succumbing to the system. Garthe possesses all those qualities, but they're . . .'

'Perverted,' Michael opined.

'Yes,' KITT went on. *'He utilizes identical capacities to achieve selfish and evil results. Of course, I'm judging only by what I can conclude from the new file on Garthe, and what you've told me yourself, of Rita Wilcox's observations. Embezzlement, fraud, assault, battery, theft, burglary, robbery, bad cheques, stolen cars, minor kidnapping, smuggling . . . Garthe had tried all these things before the age of twenty! Can that be correct?'*

'I'm afraid so. Garthe seems quite accomplished.'

'Add to that the theft of the formula for the Bonded Molecular Shell . . .' The car's electronic voice trailed away. *'I feel like I've been burgled. My shell is unique . . . or so I thought.'*

'Let's try to keep it that way.'

Somehow Michael sensed that Rita Wilcox, like the treacherous Elizabeth Bishop, had cleared out of her home.

But he made the apartment complex his first stop anyway, and was lucky enough to find a neighbour who would talk.

The neighbour was a bikini-clad lovely whose eyes ran up and down Michael several times, and found him acceptable. He did not have to fake an opening line.

'Welcome to Las Vegas,' she said, tossing her damp hair, so the sun would dry it. Her body fought to jump out of the bathing suit as she moved.

'What does that mean, exactly?' Michael said.

'Well,' she smiled, '*Exactly*, it means that Rita was here yesterday, but she's not here today. Here today, gone tomorrow – that's Las Vegas, and you're welcome to it. Get it?'

'Occasionally,' said Michael. 'Any idea where Rita lit off to?'

'That famous American destination – parts unknown.' She shrugged. 'But I still live here, and I'm diverting. My name's Vonda. If you look fast enough in the kick-dance line at the Tropicana's floor show, you'll catch my other self. You are?'

'Michael Knight.' He was thinking of his own other self, the ghostly Garthe, returned to haunt the Knight empire. 'Thanks for your help, Vonda.'

'That's nothing,' she said. 'Come on back sometime and we'll work on something worth thanking me for.' She winked comically at him as he tilted an imaginary hat, and departed.

'Anything more on the locker key?' he asked KITT once back in the car.

'*Michael, a key made from blank stock is –*'

'Right, right. What you're saying is, no news, right?'

'*I'm working on it.*' KITT paused. '*Perhaps a little computer blackjack, to pass the time while I do?*'

'No thanks. I can't afford it anymore.'

'*Cheapskate.*'

'Just head back to Caesar's Palace. It's all I can think of to do just now.'

KITT engaged AUTO CRUISE and pulled smoothly

away. By the time they had returned to Fremont Street, the main drag leading into Vegas' downtown locus of casinos, the transmission blinker went off.

'What is it?' said Michael.

'*A telex from Rio de Janiero,*' said KITT, '*dispatched via scrambler since Devon and April are out of radio range. Apparently they did not wish to use the phone.*'

As KITT spoke, the unscrambled message printed out on one of the monitor screens:

EYES ONLY / TO MICHAEL KNIGHT / FROM FLAG TOPGUY
MESSAGE:
HHG2T4 6KWSF ILW33 QTY7B9 WQP88X 5HTLLS

The printout continued for several lines, all more of the same apparently garbled mush. Devon had used Knight Industries top-line transmission code - even KITT was not capable of sifting it to readability without the proper unlocking commands, which Michael kept in his head, and which were sometimes changed on a daily basis, to frustrate computer thieves.

'Ready for decoding, KITT?'

'*Ready,*' the machine responded.

'STREETGANG TO ALMIGHTY,' Michael recited, and the words onscreen jumped into decipherability. The top-line Knight Industries scramble code included random word-breaks and decoy symbols for punctuation. It had been designed by human beings, specifically to frustrate computers, which proceeded according to ordered logical patterns.

'FLAG TOPGUY' was, of course, Devon Miles.

MESSAGE:
ELLIOT DEAD. CAUSE EQUALS OLUTA.
ELIZABETH BISHOP POSITIVE I.D. AS ELLIOT'S 'RECENT COMPANION.'
TREAD SOFTLY. D.

'Tread softly' was Devon's roundabout way of advising Michael, however unnecessarily, to be careful.

Michael read the message and sighed, as though his job was becoming too much to endure. 'This really thickens the stew, doesn't it?' he said, hands now gripping the wheel. 'If Elizabeth's *oluta* truth-cocktail worked on Devon, and if she got what she wanted from Dr Elliot, she and Garthe could *already* have the formula for the Bonded Molecular Shell in their pockets.'

'*Dr Elliot was a longstanding friend of Devon's,*' noted KITT. '*I'm sure his death has upset Devon considerably.*'

'Yeah, well, it's not good news for me, either.' He turned onto Fremont Street, joining the traffic flow headed into the heart of the gambling Mecca.

'*If it's any consolation, Michael, I may have something on the locker key.*'

'What do you mean, "may have"?'

'*I'm applying odds systems derived from my gambling studies to assess the best possibilities on where to begin searching for the subject locker most efficiently. An examination of the key's teeth reveals a particular tumbler configuration, one most frequently used on a brand of commercial locking mechanisms known as Fortress locks, which went out of business five years ago.*'

'Great. That reduces it to every locker in town with a Fortress lock.'

'*Please permit me to finish,*' said KITT. '*Tooth wear on the key indicates five-year-old tumblers – the locks were brand new when Fortress went out of business. I've cross-checked this information with the building permits and dates of construction for every commercial installation that might have purchased a quantity of such locks five years ago . . . and I've come up with two locations, a bowling alley on Desert Drive, and the municipal bus depot on Third Street. Considering the number of lockers at each location, and the public access afforded by each, I lay odds of two point seven-five-three-oh-three in favour of the bus depot. How's that?*'

'Good God,' said Michael, 'I've created a monster.'

*

With a deadpan expression, Michael counted the top row of lockers all the way across, then down. Then he multiplied. There were at least two hundred lockers . . . and the key in his hand featured no stamped number.

There was no place to begin, except at number one.

He inserted the key, withdrew it, turned it upside-down and re-inserted it. He twisted. Nothing.

This was going to be quite tedious, he realized, not to mention suspicious-looking. He was thankful for every locker that still contained its coin-released key; those he would not have to check.

When he had reached number fifteen somebody tapped him on the shoulder.

He looked around. A sharp black dude in a leather raincoat – in defiance of the heat outside – and a slouch that smiled at him, revealing gold teeth.

'Say, 'bo,' the dude said. 'Dynamite cocaine.'

'I'm the guy with the roller skates,' Michael said offhandedly. 'The guy with the cocaine is two lockers down.'

The dude's brow grew stormy. 'Hey 'bo, I'm not to buy; I'm to sell, you catch?'

'No thanks.'

The dude muttered an epithet and slunk away. There were a lot of unsavoury types making the bus depot their semi-permanent hangout. Michael could not recall the last time he had ridden on a bus – even a city bus. But he remembered that to really get in touch with the bloodstream of any city, you had to ride the buses around and rub elbows with people, even a few of the weirdos. It gave you a sense of balance. The alternative was to avoid whole sections of the city – sections that grew larger as you got older, until finally you were alone, safely bolted away in your apartment behind twelve police locks on the door.

He was now at locker number thirty. More nothing.

'Hey, you! Just what the hell do you think you're doing, boy?'

Michael turned and came up nose to nose with a burly

black security guard. He was huge, a good two hundred eighty pounds or so, and the belly that hung over his equipment belt did not deceive Michael. This guy spent a lot of his time folding and mutilating people who gave him any lip. Perspiration leaked from beneath his peaked cap, and there were huge sweatstains soaking the armpits of his blue uniform shirt.

Michael decided to play dumb *tourista*. 'I, ahh – forgot where I stowed my tennis racket. See? There aren't any numbers on the keys. Heh heh.' He grinned sheepishly.

'I saw you talkin' to Laszlo,' the guard said accusingly, 'Boy like you oughta know better.'

'I don't know him; he talked to me.'

The guard, whose anodized nametag said *Townshend*, didn't appear to be buying any of Michael's rap. 'You better pull a tennis racket out of one of these boxes, boy, and soon, or I just might have to have you detained, as a vagrant.'

'Oh, that's not necessary, officer; my car's just outside and I –'

'You're not listening,' Townshend said in his low, mellow, slightly evil voice. '*I* detain you, you don't leave the bus depot . . . except, maybe, on a stretcher.'

'Gotcha,' said Michael, sticking his key into number thirty-two.

Townshend ambled away to survey the rest of his domain, leather belt creaking. His bearlike odour hung around a while longer while Michael worked.

Locker number forty, nothing.

One hundred. 'More nothing,' muttered Michael into his comlink.

Once again, perhaps out of a mechanical surrogate for embarrassment, KITT did not respond.

Half an hour later, Michael loped out of the bus depot, mercifully avoiding both Laszlo the drug dealer and Townshend. He slumped into his bucket seat.

'Nothing,' he said. 'You know why?'

'*The odds were in favour of the bus depot*,' KITT reminded

him.

'Yeah, but at the bus depot there's a one-week limit. That's why the locker keys have no numbers. If you leave your stuff in and don't pick it up in a week, they clean out the locker, put in a new key, and auction off the stuff. It gets them a nice little nut of extra money on the side.'

'*I hadn't factored that aspect into my equation*,' said KITT disappointedly.

'Not your fault,' said Michael. 'But in gambling there are two systems – the odds, and Lady Luck. Let's see if Lady Luck will welcome us over at the bowling alley, hm?'

The fifty locker-bank at the bowling alley looked friendlier to Michael. Here, they didn't care how long your stuff might sit, locked up in the dark, as long as the mechanism captured a quarter every time the metal door was opened. The bus depot had another disadvantage, Michael now realized, as a hiding place for evidence. There was too much traffic there; too many people watching. He'd been pestered several times while trying his key – if Rita's brother Ron wanted to be secretive, the bus station would not have sufficed for his needs.

The locker bank here was tucked away in the back of the building, crowding the corridor leading to the bowling alley's restrooms. Nobody noticed anybody back in the dank hallway. A full fifty percent of the lockers still held their bronze keys.

Michael got lucky on his fourth try.

'Bingo,' he whispered into his comlink. 'Or should I say, blackjack?'

Stuffed haphazardly into the box was a blue nylon sling bag, of the type used by athletes to store gymwear. Michael did not loiter around examining its contents; he dropped the strap of the bag over his shoulder and walked out.

Once back in the car, he unzipped the bag.

'Wallet,' he said, withdrawing one, a battered brown cowhide job. 'ID is still in it. Five hundred dollars in fifty dollar bills, plus change. Photo of Rita – not very complimentary. Driver's licence.' He tossed the billfold onto the Super Dash. 'T-shirt, jeans, socks, track shoes, underwear. Sunglasses.'

'*Sounds as though Rita's brother stowed the bag in the locker as a contingency fallback, should Garthe Bishop discover what he was up to.*'

'That's the impression I get, old buddy. Here we go –' He pulled out a military-issue .45 calibre automatic, its blue steel winking in the sunlight. It was wrapped up in a battered leather shoulder holster in about the same shape as the wallet. It was fully loaded and there were two full clips clattering around on the floor of the bag. 'Now we're getting serious,' said Michael.

In the side pocket of the bag were nine cassettes, hastily labelled *A* to *I* in magic marker. In the opposite pocket there was a Sony Walkman recorder/player and a set of featherweight headphones.

Michael slipped in a tape at random into KITT's stereo system. The cabin filled up with tape hiss and interference as the tape commenced, halfway through.

'. . . 28 April . . . time hack, four-fifteen p.m. More activity at Red Bluff today. Garthe is planning something big, but there's no additional news except for one thing . . . he's been making long-distance phone calls to Africa, and getting twixes back. Thousands of dollars in communications. I don't know what it means . . .'

Twixes were teletype messages. The voice of the dead (*presumed* dead, Michael reminded himself . . . but with his growing knowledge of Garthe and the news of Dr Elliot's murder in Rio, Michael did not hold out much hope for Ron Wilcox) Ron sent a vague chill through Michael, as though the ghost of the man were speaking from the past, like Garthe emerging from history. But Ron's message could help him; it might be a warning . . . if only Michael could figure out what the man was talking about.

'I'm putting the rest of the tapes on fast-wind and plugging in your Rapid Analyzer,' he told KITT, punching the proper buttons on the digital keyboard. Touch-tone phone beeps denoted each button-push, then the glovebox-sized Analyzer slot dropped open. Its hinged black lid hung open beneath the Super Dash like a little mouth. He slotted Tape A into the player, loaded the rest into the Analyzer drawer on auto-feed, and closed the lid. Gears began to whirr efficiently. 'Start with the reference to Red Bluff – see if you can find out what, or where it is.'

'*Any sifting criteria*?' said KITT. As with any computer, a depth limit had to be imposed on the requested scan. So many billions of pieces of information were available, that without sifting criteria – specifics – KITT could swim forever through such information, without ever retrieving anything useful.

'The usual,' responded Michael. 'Start with cities and towns. Make the second-stage scan of mountains, parks, landmarks, geographical oddities.'

'*Where are we going from the bowling alley*?'

'Back to Caesar's. It's our only starting point. It's also where we saw Garthe Bishop.'

'*In work*,' said KITT. '*Michael, would you mind driving while I sort all this out*?'

'My pleasure,' he said. 'Do your stuff.'

'Sure,' said the blackjack dealer at Caesar's. 'I know Rita. We went on breaks together a couple of times.'

Michael was speaking to a good-looking Polynesian, about five foot five, with flawless nut-brown skin and inquisitive, almond-shaped eyes in deep brown. His nametag read HI! I'M TING FROM MORO BAY. 'Any idea where she is now?' he said. 'She's already cleared out of her apartment.'

'I know she requested time off, and got Sasha to take her shifts. Told the boss she was sick, but we do that all the time. No problem. Sasha'll cover for her. I saw her in here a while ago.'

'Sasha or Rita?'

'Rita, man. She looked dynamite. That's something else, too.'

'What?' Michael's eyes were already scanning the casino.

'The way she was dressed, man. Dressed to kill. So good-looking that the bosses don't even realize she's the same Rita. She used to come in here all dressed up a few months back and gamble, just to gas the bosses, and they never noticed her.' Ting pondered a moment, then squinted at Michael's face. 'You know, it's really amazing.'

Michael raised his eyebrows. Ting continued.

'Amazing that you look almost exactly like him. That Garthe dude. You sure you ain't him, just feeling me out for her whereabouts?'

'No, I'm not Garthe. Michael Knight's my name. I know, under the circumstances, that's a little difficult to prove, but I –'

'Ah, I'm just gassing you, man,' Ting smiled. 'I know you ain't Garthe.'

'How so?'

'Garthe, when I saw him, wore a diamond stud earring. His left earlobe was pierced. Unless you spontaneously regenerated an earlobe in four weeks, man, without a sign of a scar, then you ain't Garthe. A-okay?'

Michael smiled in agreement. 'You're very perceptive.' He himself had not seen Garthe's earring.

'No, man . . . very jealous. When Garthe showed up, he cut into the time I was making with Rita. She dropped me cold, man. The next day I saw why. That Garthe is loaded with dough. She was dressed so expensively; see, that's another reason nobody but us dealers caught on that it was Rita. And she was tossing away money on blackjack like it was . . .' Ting's hands worked in the air, trying to find a good simile for lavish waste.

'Don't tell me,' said Michael. 'Like it was Monopoly money.'

Ting pointed, happily, for emphasis. '*Yeah*, right! Like she was playing for matchsticks or something. And the day before, she was just one of us. And we make okay wages and tips . . . but nothing as high-class as what she was doing. So that Garthe guy gave her the clothes and the dough.' Ting chewed on that for a moment, then added, 'No. I don't favour that cat at *all*, you know?'

'You've been a terrific help, Ting,' Michael said. 'Great to meet you. I might just be able to get Garthe out of Rita's field of focus for you, if I can find her.' He drew out one of Ron Wilcox's fifty dollar bills, from the wallet still on KITT's Super Dash. 'Here's a tip in consideration for everything you told me.'

Ting turned the bill over, then folded and pocketed it. 'That's great, man, thanks. Say, Mr Knight?'

'Michael. My father's name was Mr Knight.'

'Yeah. Michael, do you ever watch detective movies?'

'Occasionally they pass before my eyes, as I'm lying in an insomniac stupor in my hotel room with just the Late Late Show for company.'

'Well, you know the scene where the private dick pays off the informant, and then the informant says, "hey, Bogie, for another bill I'll tell you where to find Lauren Bacall right now?"'

Michael laughed, mostly because Ting struck him as a good and practised capitalist. 'Now *that* scene I know by heart.' He pulled out another fifty. 'If I swap you this, can you tell me where Rita Wilcox is?'

'You got a deal, Bogie.' The fifty joined the first bill in Ting's shirt pocket. 'She's right over there.' He pointed past Michael's shoulder.

Michael caught on. 'Why, you –'

'Uh, uh, Mike, no jokes about us sneaky and insidious island people, okay? We made a deal. You jumped at it before you looked. Now we both got what we want.'

Flustered at being so easily bamboozled, Michael nevertheless thought the whole exchange amusing. 'It was worth it anyway. Got to go, Ting.' He cuffed the shorter man's shoulder fraternally. 'Have to go chase a lady.'

Ting grinned after him. 'I hear *that*, man.'

Rita was occupying the second base stool at the blackjack table where the minimum bet plaque read $100.00. She had five medium-high stacks of yellow-and-black 'bumblebee' chips in front of her. The evening dress she wore might have cost most of her chips. She wore expensive, silver high heels and her hair was done up in an elegant chignon.

She was completely transformed from the not-unattractive dealer to a real traffic-stopper. Michael was simultaneously impressed and dismayed. As he moved up behind her he checked the progress of the ongoing twenty-one hand.

Two seats over from Rita, Michael recognized the man in the cheap suit, the nervous one he'd seen abandon Rita's table when he first visited her in Caesar's. He was still perspiring heavily, and kept his hand around a pitifully small pile of one-hundred-dollar chips in front of him, like a starving squirrel hoarding nuts. He was obviously unaware that he was now playing with the same woman who, as a dealer, had cleaned him out two days previously.

Agitated, unable to cope with the pressure and speed of casino play, he glanced at his cards for the fourth time, as though he feared they would alter to a different combination if his eyes left them. 'Double down,' he said.

Michael thought the man must have a ten or eleven. Reluctantly he pushed one of his few remaining chips out into the betting circle on the green baize surface of the table.

Unconcerned, Rita nonchalantly flipped over her own cards - a jack and the Ace of Spades. Blackjack.

The sweating man had an eleven in the hole, and caught a nine. 'Twenty!' he said, triumphantly.

The dealer, who had taken no 'insurance' bets, calmly turned over her hole card next to the king she had up. It was another Ace of Spades, from the four-deck shoe.

'Blackjack,' she said, sweeping the man's bet off the table. All the blood drained from his complexion as she did. She tapped her first two fingers on the baize in front of Rita's one or two-thousand dollar bet and left it where it was, saying, 'Push'. Two blackjacks versus each other left no victor.

'You were right,' said Michael, to announce himself as he tapped Rita's shoulder from behind.

She turned, recognized him, blinked once. His reappearance did not shock or startle her. She tried to appear indifferent. She looked like a haughty rich girl, the type who gets everything she wants except true love. 'About what?'

Michael spun Ron Wilcox's driver's licence, also removed from the wallet, onto the baize so it lodged beneath the edge of her nearest stack of chips.

Her eyes took it in, then gave him a look similar to the one she'd laid on him when he'd tried to discuss business while she was working. He reached across, took a single chip from the same stack, and put it into a third betting circle, sliding onto the stool beside hers.

The female dealer shot her a questioning glance, and when she saw no objection, dealt out the hand from the shoe.

When the results were in, Michael won with a nineteen, Rita stood on an eighteen, and both the nervous man and the dealer busted. Not one word had been exchanged during play.

Michael pocketed the chip he'd won, and gave Rita the bet-chip back. 'I just paid for what it cost to find you,' he said, good naturedly. 'Let's talk. Now.'

She snorted breath out angrily, but pushed back from the table, leaving two bumblebee chips as a tip for the dealer. 'Thanks, Jody,' she said, and the dealer nodded, rapping the chips sharply on the edge of the table – to get the pit boss's attention – and then pocketed her tip, twice what Michael had given to Ting five minutes previously. The sweating man drummed his fingers on the green felt, waiting. Rita dumped her winnings into a smart-looking sequined bag threaded with liquid silver.

'Don't ever do that again,' she snarled as she and Michael walked away.

He played innocent. 'Who, me? Do what?'

'Bring up private business around public ears, damn it.'

'I just wanted to get your attention.'

'You had it yesterday. You don't have it now. You had an emergency, remember?'

'But I located Ron's stuff. The driver's licence is proof.'

'Not proof enough for me,' she returned, irritated. 'I have to leave now.'

As Michael caught her arm, there came a wild hoot from the blackjack table behind them. The nervous man in the cheap suit had won his last hand, just as Rita left the table. Jody, the dealer, rolled her eyes at the man's loud display.

'You seem to be bad luck for that guy,' said Michael, catching and holding her arm. 'Running off to see Garthe, now, my dear?'

'I may be bad luck for old Plimpton,' she said of the hooting man. 'I may turn into back luck for you if you press me about Garthe. Just leave me alone.'

His grip on her arm constricted, making red indentations in her flesh. 'Tell me what Red Bluff is,' he said, lowly, insistently.

'I don't know what you're talking about.'

'Ron did. Remember Ron? Your brother? Red Bluff and Garthe Bishop go together . . . and they both have something to do with the reason Garthe had your brother killed.'

'You don't know that,' she said, doubtfully, fear in her eyes at last. 'Thanks for your help and everything . . . but I've decided to do this my own way. I've got to go.'

This time he released her, puzzled by the bizarre personality change that seemed to have overcome her. From across the casino, Ting gave him an exaggerated shrug as she left.

Neither of them noticed Garthe Bishop, dressed in a black tuxedo, watching Michael from the threshold of the private *chemin de fer* room.

5

Garthe tilted the champagne glass up, emptying the frothy gold bubbly down his throat in a single draught. Then, with an animal grunt, he flung the glass end over end to explode into crystal dust in the suite's large, but cold, fireplace.

He walked to the suite's wet bar, his hips swaying like a panther's as he walked. As he pulled down another crystal goblet and filled it with champagne, he caught sight of his face in the backbar mirror.

A malign intellect glittered in his dark eyes. The man called Michael Knight resembled him in physiognomy, he reckoned, but the qualities Garthe thought made his own face compelling were all derived from personality, not the architecture of his flesh.

He sipped his next glass, and examined his profile. He flashed a dazzling but somehow sour smile. Yes, Michael Knight had his face all right, but it lacked the rakish moustache, the insouciant set of the cruel mouth, the devilishly sharp contrail eyebrows, the hint of king's blood one could deduce from the expression in which Garthe *held* his nose, his eyes, his mouth. The affectation of a diamond stud earring was both to flaunt his obvious wealth, and to remind the lower classes they were dealing with a member of a more privileged *caste*. Garthe's face was darkly compelling, telling tales of risky business and the pleasures of the senses. Michael Knight's face was bland, characterless. Garthe was a demi-god; Michael, just another fashion-page hunk, interchangeable with a million others.

Garthe stood and admired himself in the mirror. He had enjoyed toying with Rita, buying her, manipulating her for his pleasure, and then tossing her back out into the casino like a chunk of bait. He had given her five thousand dollars in hundred-dollar chips, a pat on her splendid behind, and orders to enjoy herself gambling. Then he had settled in, and after a few easily-won rounds of *chemin de fer*, he had stood watch, waiting for Rita to magnetize Michael Knight to her.

And sure enough, the big, dumb lunk had come, as Garthe had predicted. The elegant humour of it all amused him. He shared his laughter with his perfect mirror-image.

'You stare any harder at yourself, Garthe, and you'll turn inside-out.'

Garthe did not turn around. He watched the mirror, and the woman approaching. 'Why Mother, dear, you've not given birth to a mere narcissist. You fail to appreciate the difference between egotism and egoism.'

Elizabeth Bishop entered the room wearing an expensive evening dress and a string of diamonds. Her diamond pendant earrings counterpointed her son's stud. 'Don't be tedious, Garthe. If I were you, I'd worry more about whether Rita is in control of you . . . or you are in control of her.'

'A mere egotist,' Garthe ploughed on, knowing it annoyed Elizabeth, 'is self-involved, like a lotus-eater. An egoist, however . . . now, there is a being who knows that all human actions derive exclusively from one motivating force, and that force is self-interest.' He drained off another glass, and turned to face her. 'You slink around without making noise like some kind of alley cat, you know. Please don't sneak up on me.'

Elizabeth waved off her son's display. 'Prison not only vulgarized your taste in women, but filled your head up with inept metaphors as well, I see.' She placed her hands on her hips, all business, ignoring the glass he offered her. He drank it while she talked. 'I want Michael Knight dead. Rita Wilcox, too. My way is better. I proved that with Dr Elliot.'

Garthe laughed, harshly. 'Yes. You killed him with kindness. You slipped out of his bed and doped him while he was still dozing, his brain still reeling away in dreamland from the memorable night you gave him . . . and then you paid him back, pumping him full of sleepy-bye juice.' His gaze froze and a laugh died on his lips as if killed by a blast of liquid nitrogen. 'That was like shooting fish in a rain barrel. No style. When I killed Ron Wilcox for being a filthy little low-rent spy, I killed him elegantly. I played him out like a killer shark on a line, sharing the risk. When I hunt, dear Mother, I give the victim a fair chance to best me, and still I am always victorious. You never give your fish a chance . . . not even to flipper around, not even to breathe.'

'What about Knight and Rita?'

He shrugged it off as though insignificant. 'Rita only knows what I want her to know. She'll go the way of her departed sibling when I've tired of her as a plaything. And as soon as she serves her purpose.'

'Of reeling in Michael Knight, as you put it?'

'Mm, yes. Once again, you fail to appreciate my style, the way I'm teasing them both. Rita knows what I tell her, nothing more. Michael Knight only knows what Rita tells *him*. It's a riddle with a dead end. While he's chasing his tail, I'll deal with him at length and at my leisure. I fed Ron Wilcox specific information; made him feel as though he'd "discovered" some of my nasty secrets. That made the hunt all the more delicious. Don't you see?'

'I only see Michael Knight as a threat to our entire plan,' Elizabeth countered brusquely. She was not accustomed to being contradicted or opposed.

'Mother, don't talk like you're mouthing dialogue in a bad spy movie. There's nothing about our so-called "plan" that an insect like Michael Knight can disrupt.'

'He should be killed.'

'Now *you're* being tedious, Mother. Why are you so bloodthirsty? If you had your way, half the world would be dead. Rita will die, but that's not enough for you. Well, I have plans for Michael Knight that eclipse mere murder. How does the cliché go? "Death is too good for him."'

'He's a threat, you'll admit that much?'

'Indeed. But he's a joke, too, and that I cannot forgive,

because the joke is on me. He was created by my dead father, like Dr Frankenstein's patchwork monster, to replace me... and he cannot substitute for me any more than the shambling thing Dr Frankenstein created could pass for a stockbroker. Remember all the monster movies? The monster himself came to be called Frankenstein. He even stole his creator's name. So it is with Michael Knight. The man is a joke, and a living, breathing insult to my own existence. For him to endure, playing this part, exploiting my rightful heritage, cannot be tolerated. In a just world, he would pay for pretending to my throne. I shall make his world a just one. I shall personally send Michael Knight headlong towards a personal hell of torment. He shall take my place, the place where destiny consigned me by accident. And it will all begin tomorrow morning, Mother dear.' He toasted her with the champagne glass.

Elizabeth's interest was aroused. 'You've heard from Tsombe Kuna?'

'Just this afternoon. Things are going our way. And I'll have Goliath ready to field test by tomorrow afternoon.'

At the mention of Goliath, Elizabeth looked pleased. It was a project in which she had played a substantial role having nothing to do with mere money – she had *participated* in its realization, and that was important to her.

'I spoke to the technicians,' Garthe continued. 'The formula is ours. So tomorrow, the world of Michael Knight, and of Devon Miles' demented FLAG program, will begin to cave in, and do you know what? It'll all be an insignificant byproduct of our main interest, our principal project. That amuses me.' His eyes shone evilly. 'And now, dear Mother,' he said, 'do have a drink.'

'Wish I had a beer to cut the dust,' said Michael, tugging at the collar of his shirt. The Las Vegas heat was starting to abrade his nerves.

'*One beer would raise your blood alcohol levels beyond acceptable sobriety parameters*,' said KITT in his humourless, high-school-principal way. '*I suggest a diet cola.*'

'A diet cola?' Michael appeared horrified. 'You have no funnybone, motor mouth. A *diet* cola? That stuff always tastes like pulverized masonite mixed with Alka-Seltzer. No thank you. Besides, I'm so thirsty that one itty bitty beer wouldn't even have a chance to make it into my bloodstream.'

The Vegas strip crawled past outside the car windows. '*I've been doing some scanning on desert survival, Michael. You should read up on it. Or perhaps you'd prefer to play a little computer blackjack to pass the time?*'

'I'd rather have the diet soda.'

'*You owe me two hundred and sixteen dollars,*' the microprocessor reminded him.

'Uh – let's talk about desert survival, okay?' He gave a sickly smile to his own reflection in the mirror... and the mirror made him think again of Garthe.

'*Very well. Presume you're stranded in the desert and have to walk out on foot. Whatever you carry with you will slow you down. You are carrying a six-pack of beer and a quart canteen of water. You have a hundred miles to walk. In what order do you consume your liquid rations?*'

'Well, the six-pack weighs more than the quart canteen. Assuming 12-ounce cans, I'd drink half the six-pack – that's thirty-six ounces, or a little over a quart. Now I've got equal weight. I strap the remainder of the six-pack to my belt, and sip the water until I get really thirsty again. How's that?'

'*Not bad, Michael, but you've forgotten a crucial element. The alcohol in the beer will not satisfy your thirst; in fact, the alcohol will make you consume the water faster, because the changes it produces in your metabolism will dehydrate you. You should sip the water only; save the beer only as a last resort. Or perhaps throw the cans at something that might be killed for food.*'

'You're such a romantic, KITT,' Michael smirked. 'If I'm ever stranded in the desert, I'll try to have you around to drive me out.' Another thought struck him. 'Wait a minute! It wouldn't matter if I had a cold beer or not – *you* could do the driving.'

'*And you, of course, would do the explaining to the police when they pull you over for drinking and driving, correct?*'

'No, dummy – I'd opaque your windows first.'

'*That classifies as acting suspiciously.*'

'Sheesh! The heat must be getting to you, too. Anything further on Red Bluff?'

'*Nothing from the tapes. Since Ron Wilcox knew what it was, he never bothered to explain it to himself on the tape recorder. State Department records make obscure references to Indian land. But the Bureau of Indian Affairs claims Red Bluff – whatever it is – belongs to the government. Catch-22.*'

'What about the State Geology Department?'

'*They've supplied the most useful answer thus far – by informing us that the Las Vegas area has had many names. Before the Spanish there were the Indians . . . and several tribes all claimed the area.*'

'Maybe if we drop in on the Department of Indian Affairs personally,' Michael said. 'I'd be willing to bet Red Bluff is some tract of land the Indians got finessed out of by good old Uncle Sam . . . which is why no one is talking about it.'

As Michael spoke, KITT flashed past a junkyard of dilapidated automobiles, cars on their last legs, or wheels, or, in this particular case, wheel-rims. Dusty windshields stared, cracked and blinded, out into the traffic-flow of shining Detroit monstrosities. The aged Pontiacs and Cadillacs canted on exhausted rockers. The vinyl flags designed to attract attention to the circus of used cars were tattered and faded. There were a few newer vehicles sprinkled in amidst the junk – rolling stock, obviously sold at low price to pay for markers at some casino or other when the credit line ran out.

Above it all a paint-peeling billboard said – as loudly as it could, considering the sun-blanched, peeling paint job and dysfunctional lights – CHIEF'S A-NUMBER ONE PRE-VIOUSLY OWNED VEHICLES! Below that, a legend in over-sized script read *One Hundred Percent Real Indian*!

'On the other hand,' Michael said, making a U-turn and heading back towards the used car lot, 'we may not have to use official channels.'

'Chief' turned out to be, just as his sign claimed, one hundred percent real Indian, in this case an ancient and grinning Cherokee who still had all his teeth, and looking like he was enjoying the age of a hundred and ten. His face was a chaos of deep brown sunwrinkles, from which two coal black eyes shined out with shrewd intelligence and a knack for haggling. The Chief wore a pin-striped suit jacket that was new about three decades ago, brand-new Levis and Adidas, and an expensive-looking squash blossom around his neck. His fingers were littered with turquoise chunks mounted on hammered silver rings.

'Hey, sonny,' he said as Michael climbed out of KITT. 'You got that buyer look. You wanna buy one of the old Chief's one-owner vehicles?'

Michael smiled despite himself. He cocked his head towards an oil-leaking Chrysler mounted on blocks, wheel-less, and covered with dust. 'Who was the one-owner on this one? Geronimo's eldest son?'

'Hah, hah,' the old man cackled. 'An Indian joke, right? Good one, sonny. 'Cept that Geronimo was an Apache, and all Apaches are thieves, and you don't have to worry about stuff like gettin' scalped her at Chief's. You dig what I'm saying?' He peered around Michael to get a better look at KITT. 'So! You wanna sell that flashy piece of trash, or maybe trade it for something that'll take you places?'

'No thanks. I think I'll keep this one.'

He moved closer, to confide in Michael. 'Junk. Over-priced gas guzzler. I can give you a good deal on an economy car. I gotta Dodge Dart, a 1965, that's a real slippery honey. I save you big bucks, white man.'

Michael played along. 'I have a friend who's looking for a 1965 Dodge Dart. His name is Devon. If he could see that car, he'd be in love now.'

Chief craned around to squint at the car, as if he didn't believe his own hype, or thought he and Michael were discussing two different cars. The Dart in question had stopped Darting about sometime in 1972... at least, that was when Chief had siphoned the last of the gasoline out of the tank. He turned back, and nodded, 'Yep, that one's a slippery honey. A bargain. I bought it from a guy who needed to keep from going broke at the Four Aces. He's gonna come back and buy it back with his winnings, he told me.'

'When was that?' said Michael.

Chief looked to the sky. 'Oh... long about '78 or '79. Month of March.'

'Do you think he's coming back?'

'Sure. Ahh – who cares, right? You know how people say, "I'm not in business for my health," right? Well, sonny, I'll tell you a secret. I'm in business because I love it. The tourists and suckers love to see the doddering old Injun routine, and I give it to 'em full volume. Dumb jerks. You don't want anything in this garbage dump, so obviously you wanna talk to me, right? Answer questions, something like that. Well, for that, you have to buy a car. Even though I like your face.'

Michael chuckled. 'Okay, Chief – just how much are you *really* worth?'

He grinned conspiratorially. 'A hundred grand, easy. Maybe two. How'd you guess?'

'Vegas attracts rich eccentrics. How long have you been running this Indian used-car dealer scam?'

He shrugged. 'Five years. I hang out here when I get tired of the crap table, you know, sonny?' He waved the weight of turquoise on both hands at Michael. 'This way, some young punk like you never thinks of mugging me for my bread... because I look like I don't got a dime. You dig?' He shoved his hands into his pockets.

'Yeah. Old Howie Hughes was funny that way, too.'

'I *knew* him,' he said, and Michael believed him without question.

'Anyhow,' Michael said, gamely digging a hundred-dollar

bill out of his pocket, 'this is for a down payment on the Dart. Make the forms out to Devon Miles.'

Chief grinned and pocketed the bill. 'What do you need to know, sonny?'

'Red Bluff,' said Michael. 'Do you know what or where it is?'

He pursed his lips. 'Indian burial ground. Sacred. Really old.'

'Around here?'

'It's government land now. Restricted, I think. Old president Reagan, he Custered us out of it last year. I think there's a missile silo there now. But officially, it's "protected" Indian land . . . where Indians aren't allowed.'

'Have you got a map?'

'Nope. But if you've got one, I can show you the way to go; what roads to take. It's about a half-hour off the freeway once you get out of town.'

Michael got out a road map, and spread it out on KITT's hood.

'There she is,' said Chief. 'See the red lines? A restricted government area. But that's Red Bluff – or what Red Bluff used to be – right there. I'm sure they didn't bother to move the dead buried there.'

Chief's gnarled brown finger was pointing at the heart of a mountain.

6

The weathered sign and barbed-wire fences, though weather-worn and rusted, were to the point.

RESTRICTED GOVERNMENT LAND. ADMINISTERED BY BUREAU OF INDIAN AFFAIRS. KEEP OUT. TRESPASSERS WILL BE PROSECUTED.

Below that, some wit had scrawled '*after they are scalped.*'

It was at least a hundred and ten degrees. The sun hung hot and unmerciful in a dazzling blue sky. There was no sign of life or activity for miles, and the view went on for tens of miles.

'*The mountain's composition is mostly sandstone,*' reported KITT. '*Chalk. Iron pyrites. Alkaline soil.*'

'A lot of dead nothing,' said Michael. 'X-ray it and see what pops up.'

KITT activated his X-ray mode, and a topological schematic of Red Bluff Mountain appeared on the number two video monitor.

'*I'm registering an obstruction,*' noted KITT. '*Lead. Not a natural formation. It appears to be shielding of some kind.*' After a moment he added, '*Definitely human-fabricated. Recently, too. They appear to be lead doors. They're too large for the frames – the desert heat has made them expand. They stick when opened or closed.*'

'It's time to call Devon. Where is he now?'

'*McCaren International Airport is logged as the destination of the Knight 2000 executive jet. Devon and April should have landed half an hour ago.*'

Michael resumed his seat. 'Turn the blowers up and

refrigerate this hotbox. And get Devon.'

Within seconds, Devon's face appeared on the number one screen. He was obviously transmitting from the cabin of the jet. 'Michael. Any luck?'

'Check with your Defence Department buddy, General Maddux,' he said. 'Find out if there's any kind of secret government proving ground out at Red Bluff. Don't let him bamboozle you, like he tried to do with the Cobra Project missile dump last month. Get him to lay it on you straight. I'll wait.'

He punched on the stereo while Devon made his call, and KITT's cabin filled up with blissfully cool, conditioned air and the sounds of the intro to Muddy Waters' famous live version of 'Mannish Boy' issued from the cabin speakers. Before Muddy got to his solo, Devon called back.

'General Maddux certifies no military operation current at Red Bluff at this time. It was going to be used for an underground nuclear test site, but the voters clamped a lid on that one really quickly.'

'Sounds like he's stonewalling us, as usual. I guess it's what he gets paid for. Can you infra-red-scan the mountain at this range, KITT?'

'*I could if I had my infra-red sensor installed,*' said the car somewhat guiltily.

'What?'

'*April pulled the infra-red apparatus for maintenance a week ago. How was I to know we'd need it this afternoon? X-ray usually suffices.*'

Michael blew out an exasperated breath. 'Can you sound out the mountain with audio waves?'

'*Inefficient under these circumstances.*' After a beat, as consolation, KITT added, '*It wouldn't tell us what we need to know.*'

'Great. I think this brings us back to Rita, again.'

'Not quite, Michael,' said Devon. 'I think Elizabeth Bishop is in Las Vegas, and I intend to confront her.'

Michael entreated the image on the video screen. 'Devon,

you almost got killed the last time you two crossed paths. Don't be stupid, and don't try to become a dead hero just when I'm getting used to you, huh?'

'You underestimate the relationship Elizabeth and I once had,' said the FLAG head. 'I think she spared me because of that relationship. You know how easily Dr Elliot died.'

'Devon,' Michael protested. 'Garthe is probably lurking near her. Don't do anything until I get back to town.'

'Garthe,' nodded Devon. 'I need to confront that young upstart as well. I may give him a caning. This is my own private long shot, Michael, and it's a one man job.'

'April!' Michael shouted at the monitor. 'Make him wait till I get back - don't let him run off and do anything moronic!'

'*Oh dear,*' lamented KITT. '*I'm afraid Devon intends to... well, behave like you. He has ceased transmission.*'

The monitor screen blinked to video snow, then went dark.

Michael smacked a hand on the Super Dash. 'Come on, KITT - get us back to Caesar's, and fast. We may have to save Devon from himself!'

Devon Miles saw himself as walking casually into the lair of a dragon... but armed to the teeth.

His armament was psychological. Devon never carried weapons, and rarely pointed guns. His area of expertise was diplomacy, due process, and making right prevail by bending the systems of others to his own needs. He was rendered noble by the fact he knew Elizabeth Bishop's way was heinous and wrong. His feelings, too, had been ruffled, but he had removed the sting of the *oluta* incident in Elizabeth's Beverly Hills mansion by reducing it to irrelevancy in his mind. She was not interested in him romantically, as she had been years before, however clandestinely. She was only interested in the uses to which he might be profitably put, and in wringing the formula out of him. Why she had spared him the fate of Dr Elliot, he did not know. Devon was no expert at fathoming female psychology. Perhaps it had something to do with what she once felt for him; perhaps it had been a lucky accident.

None of that mattered now. Devon was aware he was once again sticking his hand into the viper cage – but he was now armed with the valuable knowledge that the seemingly innocuous serpents in the cage really *were* vipers, and his most valuable edge was caution.

There was another reason why Devon had privately decided to confront Elizabeth, on her own ground, by her own rules, alone. It had to do with Michael Knight.

In eighteen months with Wilton Knight's moderately successful FLAG program, Michael had become the component of direct action, with all the risks such a calling entailed. Devon's function was to remain in charge, behind the scenes. As Michael sustained both mental and physical injuries on behalf of the FLAG effort to assist those incapable of fighting 'untouchable' criminal types, Devon had gradually begun to feel an acute onslaught of what might be termed *armchair generalism.* He dispatched Michael on the missions that might some day cost the boy his existence on the planet. Rarely did Devon demonstrate his commitment to Wilton Knight's dream in such a direct, self-sacrificing fashion. Devon had begun to feel a need to put his own flesh on the line, just once, to prove he was just as capable. His psyche craved a single dose of the risk that Michael had become addicted to . . . if for no other reason than to prove to the young man that he understood the depth of such a commitment.

Devon stepped down from his vintage 1937 Bentley, one of the prides of his automobile collection. The garishly spotlit bulk of Caesar's Palace loomed like a forbidden castle, and somewhere in that maze of rooms and surly-looking people, Elizabeth Bishop, formerly Mrs Wilton Knight, waited for him.

Like the dragon, Devon thought. Or perhaps a dragon-lady. The seductress with fangs. The iron fist in the velvet glove.

At the admissions desk, Devon was given a message. He slit

open the vellum envelope and removed a card that listed the number of Elizabeth's suite . . . as he had arranged with her by telephone shortly before his conversation with Michael. Michael was probably streaking back toward Vegas in KITT at this very moment. Maybe Devon's own personal mission would be complete by then.

As he waited for the elevator – outwardly just a tall, silver-haired, sternly-featured gentleman with six generations of thick English blood backing him up – he suddenly and with shock realized that, should some kind of jeopardy confront him upstairs, he was psychologically prepared to break Elizabeth Bishop's neck with his bare hands, to snap it like a chicken bone. He knew how. And this abrupt realization of his own capacity for violence upset him. Like Melville's Billy Budd, the outrageousness of the crimes perpetrated against him was too much to bear civilly any more. The only response, his body insisted, was violence. Uncomfortably, he knew that Michael Knight would have reached the same conclusion hours, if not days, earlier. While he despised such weakness of constitution, the thought that the younger Devon might react in much the same way as Michael Knight was reassuring. What disturbed him was his blood; those six generations of stiff-upper-lip British nobility that insisted he take such unwarranted punishment with a tolerant smile.

He tapped – civilly – on the suite door, and heard movements of response from within.

She greeted him almost exactly as she had at the Beverly Hills mansion, but this time there was no intimate physical contact. 'What a lovely surprise,' she said, and her sheer cheek nearly made him choke. They both maintained their civilized façades of social form, remaining pleasant and airy, whilst inside them both, primitive animals longed for bloodletting.

She was, of course, dressed for homicide. Another few brownie points on the psychological violence scale, thought Devon. She was elegantly bejewelled and enticingly clad. Her legs, supple from hours of aerobics workouts, flashed in and out of the dramatically cut gown. Elizabeth had always preferred gowns, the way the wealthy never prefer anything less than vintage champagne – the kind of vintage that has more to do with the numbers on the price tag than the numbers of the year of vintage.

The suite was – just as naturally – one of Caesar's Palace's best-appointed. First class.

The ubiquitous wet bar waited in a corner of the room formed by two walls of windows converging. The floor-to-ceiling curtains were drawn back, and twelve floors below, Las Vegas glittered, billions of watts of brilliance pushing back the night.

She moved to the bar. 'Something for you, Devon, dear?' Every movement of hers seemed rehearsed; every stance was a conscious pose.

'How kind of you,' he said. 'Perhaps a belladonna cocktail with a bit of arsenic on the side? Or a sodium pentothal highball?'

She emitted a high, fluting laugh. He did not let it effect him.

'I want you to stop the insanity you and Garthe are planning,' he said.

'Very dramatic,' she said, caustically. 'You know, Devon, in many ways you remind me of Wilton. The staunch do-gooder. The flair for overblown hyperbole. Working for FLAG has put too much sugar in your coffee, if you ask me.'

He pressed on, implacably. 'I flew to Rio de Janiero. I identified Dr Elliot's corpse. And I know you were there. And it seems you got what you wanted.' His composure crumbled a bit when he remembered the golf excursions he once shared with Kyle Elliot. Another friend gone, another enemy gained...

'Oh, Devon, don't be such a straitlaced fuddy. I dropped in on Kyle in Rio; we had a drink, he made a pass at me, and that was it. We were old friends as well. He died after my visit. His heart was as bad as Wilton's. I'd always warned him about it.' She poured herself an icy-cold martini, super-dry, the merest hint of vermouth, and the subject of Kyle Elliot, for her, was shrugged away with the action.

His friend's life, thought Devon. A drop in the bucket. 'How did you slip it to him, Elizabeth?' he ventured coldly. 'Surreptitiously, in a drink? Or did you offer him your body and make him drink it knowingly? Or did you threaten the information out of him, and then give it to him by force?'

'Dear Devon,' she said again. 'Kyle's death had more to do with a rotten, cholesterol-clogged heart than an exotic African poison.'

'I said nothing about a poison.' A slight smile touched his lips. Elizabeth had trapped herself.

'You're such a charming man,' she said. 'But so suspicious. Practically paranoid.'

'You're forgetting that you're talking to a survivor of another of your deadly *digestifs*,' said Devon. 'I don't intend to spar with you further. You've stolen the formula for the Bonded Molecular Shell. I know all about Red Bluff. You must cease the course you're on. Isn't that enough?'

A low, poisonous voice came from the bedroom, from behind Devon. 'You starched old fool,' it said. 'Haven't you learned by now that my mother never gets enough? That she is acquisitive, the way a black widow acquires dead husbands for food?'

Devon turned, and for the first time in more than ten years, stood face to face with Wilton Knight's son, Garthe. He had to fight the disorienting notion that he was dealing with Michael Knight, behind the moustache and diamond stud earring. The eyes were all wrong. They glinted, feral and hungry. Garthe had inherited his mother's taste for accumulation – he wanted everything that was not his, or that he had not destroyed.

'I believe you two know each other,' said Elizabeth, calmly sipping her drink.

Garthe strode in from the suite's dark bedroom, carrying a polished ebony cane with a diamond-encrusted, beaten silver head. He still wore his tuxedo, and Devon saw that the tie was a typical Garthe touch – it was made of black leather.

'I knew him before the moustache,' said Devon. 'Before his . . . African experience.'

'Oh, by all means, let's dance,' said Garthe, ambling to the bar. 'Let's jab each other socially, shall we? You are a crude, ignorant do-gooder, Mr Miles. Amazingly like my late father, corporate mercenary and buccaneer that he was. A hypocrite. A fool. And soon to be as dead.'

Elizabeth handed Garthe another dry martini.

'I've come purely as emissary,' said Devon. 'To try and reason you out of your planned course of action.'

Garthe snorted a harsh laugh. 'Isn't that what the enemy always does on the brink of utter defeat? "Tries to reason" with the victor?'

Devon shook his head, sadly. 'You really don't see the madness of what you're doing.' Now he felt rather sorry for both of them.

Garthe approached. He seemed held together by a thousand tightly-strung wires, all tied to a central post whose structural integrity was less than a sure bet. His words spat forth like bullets from a gun. 'Let me introduce you to reality, as a victor,' he snarled. 'I am about to defeat you, and, like the villains in the spy movies I so dearly adore, I'm entitled to a speech, and the speech is this: I am going to crush you, and your pathetic Foundation for Law and Government, because you both offend me. And I will squash Michael Knight like a cockroach. Yes, I know all about Michael Knight – he is the joke you helped perpetrate on me.' His eyes were cold and alien now, like the gaze of a hungry iguana. 'Oh, I've seen the photos. The surgery I can guess at. You and Wilton Knight must have laughed and laughed – Garthe was a failure, so let's build a *new* Garthe! Wilton Knight was a crusty old peggo; he thought he could buy anything – even the silence of his emotionally bankrupt ex-wife.'

'Be careful, little boy,' warned Elizabeth. Clearly there had been some feuding going on between these two power-hungry animals. 'Do watch that.'

'Shut up, Mother,' he snapped. Devon was amazed when Elizabeth flinched and backed down. He realized now that only someone with Garthe's measure of clear insanity could throw a scare into her.

Garthe raised his cane and tapped Devon on the solar plexus with it. 'Do you know that she and my father slept together only twice? Twenty-eight years ago. And here I am, like a nightmare come true for Wilton Knight's marital shortcomings. He never wanted a wife, he wanted an heir. She was a walking incubator, nothing more.'

Elizabeth had buried her face in her hands.

'And just because the heir didn't turn out like all Wilton Knight's brain boys planned doesn't mean that he won't collect his due,' grinned Garthe. 'FLAG is a fantasy. Fuelled by delusions perpetrated by fools. As rightful heir to the Knight name, I shall destroy FLAG. You. Her. Michael Knight. And when the smoke clears, the only thing that will remain will be me.'

He emptied his glass, and, as before, hurled it violently against the wall, making everybody jump.

'You're quite insane,' Devon suggested mildly.

'You're crazy to think you can go on, old man,' Garthe returned. 'You've served your purpose, you're *extinct*. Why are you even wasting your time? Don't tell me – it's because you're an altruist, dedicated to the higher ideals of FLAG. What rot. A misguided old fool, a stupid young fool, and a car, and a collection of microprocessors. Not even your wonder car will survive what I have planned. As usual, I have something bigger – and better – in mind.'

'Machines of war, no doubt,' said Devon. 'Using the Bonded Molecular Shell.'

'This conversation has become redundant,' said Garthe. 'You are dismissed. We already know you were not followed. Be grateful that I've given you a few hours more of life – consider it a gift from the new order. Now get out of here.'

'I suppose if I bring anyone back, you'll already be gone.'

Garthe's expression indicated that this was correct, but he

said, 'But how could I go anywhere? I don't exist, remember? I'm a bad dream. I'm your worst nightmare. And you have no more time in which to wake up. Now I shall become the reality . . . and you shall become the forgotten dream.' He reconsidered the beaten Elizabeth, waiting mutely by the bar. 'Leave us. I have some filial comfort to dispense. And remember this – you're already dead. What you see in the mirror is just a walking ghost.'

Then he laughed, and somehow that was the most horrible part of the entire afternoon.

7

Frustrated, Michael cruised the Strip for what seemed like the millionth time in the past three days. He was bound not for Caesar's, which Devon Miles had just left (although neither he nor April would be aware of Devon's scrapeless getaway for an hour or so), but for the Flamingo. The recently-remodelled hotel currently boasted the most expensive single-night-rate suites in Las Vegas, and Rita Wilcox was installed in one of them.

Her call had been peculiar, he thought. Almost contrite.

'*It seems as though the young lady has had a change of mind,*' said KITT.

'You mean change of heart,' said Michael, surprised that KITT had somehow divined his thoughts.

'*As you use the expression, Michael, I see no fundamental difference. Do you consider the heart to be the same as the mind, metaphorically speaking?*'

'Well,' he said, turning into the Flamingo's underground garage, 'yes and no.'

'*Michael,*' said KITT with patient weariness, '*the phrase "yes and no" counters the precision of the English language.*'

'That's why I like it,' said Michael. 'Imprecision is a precise skill.'

'*I don't understand a word you've just said.*'

He shrugged and delivered his punchline: 'Same difference. Any word from Devon?'

'*April says no as of thirty seconds ago.*'

'Okay, keep me posted on the comlink. Here I go again, into the jaws of doom.'

'I'm sorry I acted the way I did,' Rita said . . . contritely, as

Michael had predicted.

He stood in the middle of the Flamingo's Suite 101 – a sybarite's delight, a garden of earthly pleasures, a vast chamber sunk in deep pile carpeting and golden fixtures, a place where the closets were as big as bedrooms, the bedrooms as lush as the inside of a passion fruit, and the parlour as big – apparently – as half a basketball court. There was a three-level, sunken circular 'conversation area', a marble-topped bar ten feet long and fully-stocked, the usual floor-to-ceiling picture windows with motorized curtain tracks, and enough plush sofas, loveseats and ottomans to seat all the middle management executives of Getty Oil. Michael tried not to gawk, but the sheer extravagant excess of the room's furnishings defeated him.

He estimated the worth of just the jewellery hanging from Rita at fifteen grand in diamonds and 24-carat gold – cork-screw earrings with black pearl drops, delicate ear cuffs, a solid gold chain of rectangular open links that just had to be a gift of Garthe's, the type to prove ownership – and her clothes at a cool five hundred bucks in designer jeans, original-design shoes and a figure-hugging silk cowl-neck. She had the look of a rich man's mistress all right.

Rita moved to the bar, hips swaying distractingly for Michael. She knew how attractive she was, and something gave a thud in his chest. She poured herself a ginger ale in a frosted, silvered cocktail glass, then raised her eyebrows to Michael.

'Beer,' he said, recalling his earlier conversation with KITT.

She brought him a bottle of dark Heineken and moved back towards the carpeted pit of the living room.

'Amongst other things,' she continued, 'I was angry at you for dashing off right at the moment you'd given me some hope about Ron. I was ready to grasp at any straw. You offered one, then yanked it away. So I got upset.'

'I can tell,' Michael said, indicating his beer bottle. 'No glass for me.'

Her mood lightened. 'I really felt powerless when you cut out on me.'

'But I'm back now,' he said. 'I came as soon as you phoned April.'

'I just felt that no one, you know – *cared* whether Ron was alive, dead, missing, murdered, or anything.' She sipped, leaving pale lip-prints on the rim of the silvered tumbler.

'That explains your anger at me,' Michael nodded. 'But it doesn't explain the jump from blackjack dealer to one hundred dollar tipper, or from that cinderblock filing cabinet to this one-thousand-dollar-per-night funhouse.' He sipped, pacing strategically around her in the carpeted pit. 'So you decided to punish Garthe Bishop by going to bed with him?'

'Nobody punishes Garthe,' she said sullenly. 'If they could, I'm sure he'd get off on the pain. I did it to find some rock-hard proof he killed my brother.' She glared up at him. 'It's a talent I know how to use. I bet I got further than you did – unless the tapes gave you a lead you haven't mentioned.'

'Dead ends,' said Michael. 'Mysteries. Locked doors in the desert.'

'Okay, so you're in no position to judge me.' She crossed her legs and folded her arms defiantly. Michael knew that it had taken a double measure of courage for her work against Garthe by becoming his mistress. Rita apparently had the backbone for the nerve-wracking approach she'd chosen; the stamina to deceive Garthe – or try to.

'So have you got your proof?'

'Yes and no.'

Michael smiled. 'A friend of mine would wince to hear you say that.'

'The same friend who advised you to double down every time you got an eleven, right?' she said, unaware that she was right. 'As I recall, you pulled a thirteen. Not good enough.'

'Well, I'm better at detective work than blackjack.'

'We'll see. I overheard a bit last night that I can't figure out. Maybe you can.' She closed her eyes, reconstructed the scene in her mind. 'Garthe answered the phone in the bedroom, then hung it up, got out of bed, and took the call in here. I pretended I was asleep. When he was out the door, I picked up the phone and listened in. The first thing he said was, "the shell is ready." Does that have any meaning for you?'

Michael nodded slowly. 'The Bonded Molecular Shell.'

'Apparently, somebody or something named Tsombe Kuna is arriving here tomorrow morning, early. At noon, Garthe is supervising some sort of demonstration.'

'Where?'

She shrugged. 'Not sure. Sorry.'

His comlink peeped and he answered it. 'Hang on a sec,' he told Rita.

'*Michael, April reports that Devon just walked in the door at the trailer*,' came KITT's voice from the tiny speaker grille. '*He is intact.*'

'Any news?'

'*More information on Elizabeth Bishop's involvement. Two weeks following the PALM raid that freed Garthe and Tsombe Kuna from the Tongo M'Kimbe death camp, the government official who jailed Garthe for running guns to the Mau Mau insurrectionists committed suicide.*'

'Sure he did,' said Michael.

'*The official had accepted bribe money to "push through" the leases to the land Garthe and Kuna later mined for the diamond value, and still own. The official's name was Komo Timbaru. For a short period of time, Timbaru was known to have a white mistress. The woman fits Elizabeth Bishop's description.*'

'So she greased Garthe out of prison, and Garthe used the leases to set up their cash base.' The operation had been slick. All events had transpired in a matter of weeks.

Rita overheard, and gave Michael an expression that told him most of KITT's information did not make any sense to her.

When KITT signed off, Michael said, 'Did Garthe say anything else at all during the call last night?'

'I had to hang up before he came back to bed,' she said.

'Resume my pretence of sleep, you know, all's well. As it was he woke me up on purpose anyway. But he did say one other thing: "Goliath is born." '

Michael repeated the phrase. 'Certainly sounds like it's all coming together for him tomorrow morning. Are you *sure* there's no way to fix Garthe's location?'

She hesitated. 'I could invite him back here, tonight.'

'I can't ask you to do that, Rita.' He genuinely felt compassion for her.

'No sweat,' she said with false lightness. 'I signed on for this trip, I'll take the knocks. It's the one sure way to nail him. You just make sure you don't lose him in the morning, when he leaves.' Her words seemed bitter but her mood was one of determination.

'Thanks.' He squeezed her hand, and before he knew it she swept him into her arms.

'Thank me this way,' she said, and kissed him full on the mouth, surprising him.

He held her that way for a while, letting her get a psychic battery charge from his nearness. As they embraced, he saw their reflection in the window glass, and he thought of her embracing Garthe, later that day. Dr Jekyll and Mr Hyde had connected up again, he thought. Garthe was haunting him like an evil *doppelganger*, like KARR, the negative version of KITT, had intruded on their lives several months earlier. There was an overload of *déjà vu* to this whole investigation, only this time the antagonist was not a renegade version of FLAG's proud machine, it was a sinister duplicate of FLAG's own maverick pilot for that machine.

Michael had KITT. Garthe had 'Goliath'. Whatever Goliath was. He didn't want to think about it just now.

Instead, he kissed Rita back, inhaling the scent of her hair, drowning in her closeness.

Michael was thankful upon seeing Devon's face fill up KITT's number two video monitor. His FLAG mentor looked alive and well. He had survived his confrontation with

Elizabeth, and, as Michael learned, had watched Garthe chink the seemingly indestructible woman's armour. Michael's immediate impulse was to tear out for Caesar's Palace in the hope of apprehending – or clamping a tail on – the pair.

'I'm sure they've absconded by now,' said Devon. 'It's fruitless to return there.'

Michael related the news regarding Garthe's demonstration for Tsombe Kuna, and Rita's assistance.

'It looks like, with all our resources,' said Devon, 'that we are faced with the most horrible task of all – waiting till tomorrow morning.'

'No,' said Michael. 'Get General Maddux back on the phone and squeeze him about those lead doors in the middle of Red Bluff. In case that doesn't work, have April prepare KITT's infra-red unit. I'm going back out to Red Bluff today, before Garthe shows up back at the Flamingo.'

'In work,' Devon said, and signed off.

'Let's go get your Superman vision back,' he said.

'*I'm afraid reinstallation of my infra-red mode might allow us to see something we'd rather not see, at this stage,*' said KITT.

'Don't be squeamish, pal,' said Michael. 'Bad news is part of our business.'

'*And no news is good news,*' returned the car.

'Ah, but that phrase is an insult to the precision of the English language,' Michael said with glee.

KITT was silent for the rest of the drive.

8

The implacable sentry did not have to hear or see the approaching limousine; he knew it was coming. He would have known it even if no one had given him advance word – that was his function. To be aware.

The limo was long and low, riding close to the ground because of the weight of its armour plating. Its windows were mirrored mysteries; its chrome trim shone fiercely in the desert heat. A pallid cloud of dust floated in its wake as it neared the sentry's position.

The sentry snapped rigid, holding his Uzi machinegun at port arms, using his free hand to adjust the beret on his head, which was a deep maroon punctuated by a palm-leaf insignia. They were called Red Berets as commandos, but their headgear was closer to the colour of dried blood than scarlet.

The property was posted PRIVATE INDUSTRY for ten miles in every direction around the sentry's checkpoint. That meant trespassing was frowned upon. In fact, the sentry knew that interlopers were swiftly prosecuted to the full extent of the law – the ones that survived, that is. Behind the sentry was a high-voltage security fence. He knew it was powered up because he had seen a sparrow alight on the mesh links half an hour earlier. It had been flash-fried on contact, and dropped to the sand in a smouldering mess of blackened meat and scorched feathers. Beyond the fence was the warehouse, and in the warehouse was a mystery. It was not the sentry's business to know, so the warehouse's contents were irrelevant to him. He stood guard. He did it quite well.

The heavy black limo came to a gravel-crunching halt one foot from the unmoving sentry's locked knees. He saluted briskly.

The chauffeur of the limo keyed down the driver's-side window and allowed the sentry to peek inside. Satisfied, the sentry turned and unlocked the gate after giving the signal to another guard on the opposite side. The killing current was switched off, the gate rolled back, and the limo slid into the compound, pulling to a turned-in stop before the warehouse doors.

Doors popped efficiently open and several more Red Berets climbed out bearing automatic weapons. Then a Beret with three gold hashmarks on his cap followed; this was a Chiruwi, one of Garthe Bishop's elite bodyguards. He toted a lethal Sodov shotgun, its bores designed to distribute shot in a pattern that would kill as many people in as short a period of time as possible.

The ebony cane with the diamond-cluster head next extended out of the car to touch ground, with Garthe Bishop right behind it. He looked disapprovingly up at the sun and drew heavy sunglasses from a shirt pocket.

Next came a sandalled black foot, above which fluttered luridly coloured tribal robes of high rank. Tsombe Kuna was a squat and muscular man with a broad-planed African face and a dignified manner that offset the outrageousness of his native costume. Around him the Red Berets uttered their harsh military bark and stomped gleaming black boots, coming to respectful attention.

Kuna gazed unblinkingly at the desert sun. 'Six thousand miles from the sedge, to travel to this place,' he said in a mellow basso voice. 'And I feel as if I know it. I know all deserts well, Garthe, my brother.'

'The deserts of the Transvaal and the deserts of the United States each hold their special charms, my brother,' Garthe said, invoking his right of intimacy, of familiarity with Kuna. He was one of the few white men permitted to address the revolutionary leader in this fashion, and they often spoke in such riddles, as though they were sages. 'All deserts evoke respect. You must respect them or they kill you dispassionately, and nothing is so tragic as a death without passion.'

Kuna grinned behind mirrored sunglasses, exposing large yellow canines. 'But a death with passion?'

'Is a planned death, and is to be savoured. I think you'll enjoy the little demonstration I've planned for you. It represents just the right combination of practicality and . . .' Garthe's gaze wandered to the hills, to the road beyond the gate, as though he was searching or waiting for some additional member of their entourage to arrive. 'And irony. We shall see.'

'I have no doubt I will be impressed.'

Garthe smiled his viper's smile. 'Nor do I, my brother.'

The warehouse portals cranked slowly back on chain-driven tracks as they approached. Within, Kuna could see the sunlight bouncing back from an enormous chromed grille. Banks of high-powered headlights were mounted on each side of the grille, like the multiple eyes of a tarantula.

Garthe rushed ahead, eager to unveil his accomplishment personally. He checked his watch. 'The final layer of the Bonded Molecular Shell has achieved the tertiary stage of its crystallization. The first two stages are the longest and most laborious; they are the reason I've dawdled so long in Las Vegas.'

Tsombe Kuna looked up and up. The centre of the silver grille – which looked like a hungry mouth – threw back his reflection. He was looking at the front of a truck, and the truck was nearly two storeys tall.

'Meet Goliath,' said Garthe.

Their eyes grew accustomed to the darkness, and more details were revealed. Goliath was a massive tractor-trailer rig, larger than the largest Kenworth long-hauler. The cab was littered with chrome and orange bubble lights. The flawless black surface of the Bonded Molecular Shell glittered like dark, still water, like black diamonds, like polished ebony.

'By now the shell has achieved maximum hardness,' said Garthe. 'Kumenya?'

The Chiruwi guard stepped forward.

Garthe directed the man's attention to the side of the truck, by the driver's step-up door. 'Fire at the side, point blank.'

Kumenya complied instantly, whipping up the Sodov weapon and cutting loose with both barrels. The report was deafening, echoing off all the metal in the warehouse, and the speed with which the Chiruwi fired on command was a little frightening. The Sodov used dense-pack, high-velocity shot that resembled steel-jacketed lead balls an eighth of an inch in diameter. The charge was powerful enough to blow the truck door off the hinges; Kumenya was one of the few men in the room who could fire the Sodov without getting his arm kicked from the shoulder socket with recoil.

The salvo struck the side of the truck with a *planging* sound and a small cloud of white smoke.

'See for yourself,' Garthe said proudly.

There was a blast pattern of white smudges all over the truck door, but when Kuna stepped forward and touched them with his fingers, expecting depressions, he discovered that they were the powdered residue of the heavy shot, which had totally disintegrated on striking the Bonded Molecular Shell. Under the sticky powder of vaporized metal the surface was smooth and virgin, uninterrupted.

Kuna looked around the truck. It seemed to stretch back into the darkness of the warehouse, as though it was growing ever more massive while they stood there, awed.

He turned back to Garthe. 'I am impressed, my brother,' he said with his broad African smile.

'*Gunshots, below,*' said KITT.

Michael's eyes jumped to the video monitors, which featured staggered views of the warehouse and the perimeter. 'Inside?'

'*Yes. I cannot assess who or what might have been shot, however.*'

'We'll sit tight. Now that we have some idea of what kind of stakes Garthe is playing for, let's permit him to make the next move.'

'*I don't want any more nasty surprises today,*' complained

KITT.

The car was referring to the events of that morning. Before staking out the Flamingo at dawn in order to tail Garthe to his desert destination, Michael had made the long haul back to Red Bluff, equipped with wirecutters, lock picking tools, and KITT's re-installed infra-red sensing device. April had done a rush job on this last, but it was calibrated through KITT's main sensor and fairly discreet. Once they had ascertained the barbed wire fencing featured no cleverly concealed alarm system, Michael clipped the barrier apart and drove KITT to within a hundred yards of the gigantic double doors of lead set in the mountainside.

Before proceeding further, he phoned Devon.

'Any word from General Maddux on what he's got hidden inside Red Bluff?'

'No,' responded Devon's video image. 'In gambling-parlance, Maddux is giving us a poker face on the whole affair . . . which, to me, indicates there is something there to cover up. He obviously thinks he can keep us in the dark with lead doors.'

'We'll see. Literally. I'm transmitting the image to your terminal.'

'Proceed,' said Devon.

'Fire it up, KITT,' said Michael. 'Let's see what all the commotion might be about.'

The configurations that appeared on the sceen were unrecognizable to Michael.

'Shore Attack Dees,' Devon seemed to say in astonishment.

'Say again?' said Michael, confused.

'Shore Attack D's,' enunciated Devon. 'Military short-form for the designation rolling up on your screen now.'

Devon's face disappeared and was replaced by computer lettering.

SHORE ATTACK D
EQUALS

SHOR * ATTAC * D . . . OR
. . . *SHO*RT-*RA*NGE *T*HERMONUCLEAR *TAC*TICAL *D*EVICE DEFENCE DEPARTMENT CONTRACT 12-B-0007546-C6-73883 MANUFACTURED IN LEBANON, INDIANA.
* A SHORT-RANGE MISSILE DELIVERY SYSTEM INCORPORATING NUCLEAR-TIPPED SINGLE WARHEAD PAYLOAD DESIGNED AS BORDER-TO-BORDER DEFENCE EXPEDIENT, I.E., CLOSE-RANGE LOCALIZED LOW-KILOTON NUCLEAR SURFACE COMBAT.

'Holy cow,' said Michael. 'I didn't even know we *had* these things.'

'They were first proposed in the 1960s,' came Devon's disembodied voice, 'when the Cold War has hotting up and it looked like the only answer was to atomize selected portions of Europe.'

'Nuclear combat, toe-to-toe with the Russkies,' Michael said, trying to remember that far back.

'Now, of course, we've overrun most of Western Europe with Pershing-II and Cruise Missiles,' said Devon. 'The SHOR-ATTAC has been obsolete for fifteen years.'

'But that doesn't mean they aren't still stockpiled,' realized Michael. 'And here they are. Devon, this is more serious than just Garthe's vendetta against Knight Industries!'

'Offhand, I'd speculate that Garthe plans somehow to employ the Bonded Molecular Shell to penetrate the stockpile and get the missiles into the hands of Tsombe Kuna's Pan-African Liberation Movement.'

'After which Kuna will turn any country that opposes him into a radioactive garbage dump,' said Michael. 'But the stockpile has got to be heavily safeguarded.' Then the truth dawned on him. 'A tank couldn't get in . . . but KITT might be able to.' The last puzzle piece fell into place in his mind, and the resultant picture was spectacularly ugly.

After that, the imperative had been to stick to Garthe

Bishop's tail, and Michael had got back to the Flamingo in a hurry, arriving just before dawn. Garthe's limousine was checked into the parking garage – without a guard inside it, Michael noticed. Tickling the trunk lock open had been fairly easy; he secreted a tiny pinhead homing device just beside the tail-light mount on the right side. It would show up on KITT's video monitor street-map overlay as a blinking green set of crosshairs . . . and it was by this method Michael had tracked Garthe into the desert, to the warehouse location, at just past high noon.

'*Registering a heavily-horsepowered diesel engine starting up,*' KITT reported, breaking Michael out of his reverie.

'Okay, pal – let's see what Uncle Garthe has in store for us.' He imagined all kinds of horrific tanks and missile-carrying vehicles with treads.

The last thing they both expected to see was a huge truck, gleaming black, like a hyperthyroidal supermarket delivery vehicle, rolling ponderously out of the warehouse, the top of its cab barely clearing the hangar-sized doors.

'*Getting conflicting readings now,*' said KITT, obviously dismayed by the sight. '*Reading both diesel output and some kind of supercharger. The cab is shielded against scanning – indicating that the Bonded Molecular Shell is not the only coating protecting the exterior surfaces.*'

'Garthe is even more paranoid than the US government when it comes to a little spy-eye,' said Michael, thinking of the lead doors back at the missile stockpile. That led him to an unfocused contempt for all missile delivery systems. It certainly seemed as though he and KITT spent a disproportionate amount of their time – squandering it, really – by keeping various missile systems out of the hands of freebooters. There had been the gunrunning incident with the *Corazones de Piedras* last year, and the more recent set-to with missile mercenaries led by one Eduardo O'Brien, recently deceased. And now the SHOR-ATTACs . . . and what was quite pointedly the vehicle intended to ferry them out of the stockpile at Red Bluff. 'That truck is enormous,' said Michael, watching it both through the front window and the monitor screens. 'Even money says that that monster is "Goliath".'

'*No wager*,' responded KITT. '*Exterior measurements indicate that the truck is four times my length and approximately two storeys high. A flexible estimate of its gross weight is fourteen tons.*'

'And all of it coated with the Bonded Molecular Shell.' Michael whistled between his teeth.

'*Michael, I respectfully suggest we get Devon to alert General Maddux to the impending raid on the missile stockpile. More to the point, I think we should put as much distance between ourselves and that behemoth as is – you will pardon the expression – humanly possible.*' When Michael didn't respond right away, KITT's vox-box blinked with nervousness. '*Michael?*'

'Forget about Maddux,' snorted Michael. 'We waste a lot of time dickering with Army idiots who refuse to admit they've got dirty little nuclear bombs stashed all over the country. Like those Stiletto rockets Eduardo O'Brien got his paws on – those didn't "exist" either, officially. Maddux's way lies red tape and madness. Let's concentrate on pulling Garthe's plug instead.'

'*How? Do you see the size of that thing?*' KITT began to sound more and more like an insecure kid about to have his first run-in with the school bully.

'I'm working on it,' said Michael.

Just as he spoke, a violent explosion went off behind them, followed by three more blasts. Chunks of earth disgorged, smoke rose and all of a sudden, the hillside slid down to seal off the road behind them.

'Bushwhack!' Michael shouted, flinching from the noise of the explosions but trusting in KITT's impenetrable skin to keep him intact. 'KITT, we've been ambushed!'

'*There is no longer an egress from this valley*,' KITT reported dolefully. '*The road out has ceased to exist.*'

'Great. I think Rita Wilcox might have sold us out, old buddy.'

'The truck has left the compound and is accelerating up the access road. It is edging near 120 miles per hour.' With a sense of impending doom, KITT added, *'It seems to be targeted on our current position, and will get here in a little under fifty seconds.'*

9

Garthe Bishop's Red Berets had rapidly set up a series of gaily coloured umbrellas and a portable bar for the comfort of Tsombe Kuna. The soldiers squinted under the sun's glare as Tsombe sipped an iced Perrier with lime... and watched Garthe bring Goliath forth from the warehouse.

As the truck rolled free of the hangar doors, Garthe had given a radio signal to the Berets, who set off the series of explosive charges planted in the access roadway that morning, and designed to cause the hillside to collapse into the road, sealing off retreat. He knew all about Michael Knight's homing device – he'd detected it in his limousine early that morning – and decided to play with his fish a bit before reeling him in. Michael had been under the scrutiny of a pair of Red Berets with binoculars even since his arrival at Garthe's 'test site'... and now his escape from the canyon had just been blocked.

Oh, Garthe thought, revenge was going to taste smooth and sweet.

Michael Knight, his imperfect duplicate, his faulty clone, was trapped at one end of the canyon. When he realized his predicament, he would charge into the fray, trusting in his armoured car, the Knight Industries Two Thousand, which symbolized to Garthe the entire FLAG program begun by his late father, and which he despised. He, Garthe, was better than Michael Knight. And his creation, the mind-bogglingly huge Goliath, dwarfed the machine Knight piloted. It was an elegant comparison for Garthe because the order that had denied him, had thrown him out, had caused him to end up in a stinking Tongo M'Kimbe death camp, was now cast into shadow – *his* shadow. He had risen from that swamp grave like an avenging demon, to blot out the existences of those who had betrayed him.

He pushed Goliath into acceleration. The digital speedometer touched the century mark, and a few seconds later, he read a steady 120 miles per hour. The military-issue supercharger inside Goliath's powerhouse had been supplied through the kind offices of Tsombe Kuna's African mercenary connections. Now Kuna, his spiritual brother, was about to get back some of the butter he had never denied Garthe. He was going to witness firsthand a demonstration of the Bonded Molecular Shell that could make his tanks, his jeeps, his transport vehicles invulnerable – even his soldiers, once the process was applied to light-weight fibreglass body armour.

It was not coincidental that the demonstration would also have the byproduct of slapping FLAG's face. Garthe had sensed the strategy of his enemies and had planned accordingly. This would not only be vengeance for himself, but for his mother, who had also been cast out. He recognized his obligation to her; without her, he could not have gained access to the formula for the Bonded Molecular Shell so professionally. Elizabeth Bishop believed in her son – that was the crucial difference between her and her late ex-husband. It was the reason, to Garthe, that Wilton Knight lay mouldering in a grave, and Elizabeth remained vibrantly alive.

He reached to the dashboard and punched up a sophisticated targeting computer. On a monitor screen the valley ahead jumped into video-game relief. By negative-reversing the frequency of the homing device Michael had planted in Garthe's limousine, the device now aided Garthe in pin-pointing KITT's position. The black street machine sat at the far end of the valley, unmoving. He hit another button, and the yardage to the objective began to click speedily off on a digital readout.

Back at the test camp, Tsombe Kuna watched, amused, through a pair of highpowered PAX-3 binoculars. There were also video cameras, manned by several Red Berets, recording the test for reference.

The blip on the monitor screen had begun to move toward Goliath's position, slowly at first, thirty, forty miles per hour, gaining speed.

Garthe slammed his hand on the huge steering wheel in triumph. '*I knew it*!' he shouted to himself. 'I knew he couldn't resist! The fool!' He began laughing, loud and hard, suffused in his own sense of victory and the thrill of vengeance.

Ahead of him on the road, the black dot that was KITT began to grow. Garthe reached up and yanked the nylon cord hard, and a triple-horn diesel blare filled up the valley with its echoes. It sounded like the battle call of some impossibly huge prehistoric monster.

'*I repeat, for clarity*,' KITT said with a hint of desperation. '*Four times my length. Two storeys high. Fourteen tons. It has my protective shell. Michael, that thing is bigger than we are. I strongly suggest a strategic withdrawal.*'

'Nothing doing,' said Michael grimly, putting the car into gear and accelerating down the road. 'We're going to take him on.'

'*Michael, this is a foolhardy and reckless course of action. You might get us both killed.*'

He coughed out a bitter little laugh at that. 'KITT, if you're not going to help me, then shut up.'

He negotiated the final foothills curve and moved onto the straight doing seventy.

He knew it would be impossible to explain to KITT just why he was compelled to leap into a full scale confrontation with Garthe and Goliath, but the urge was strongly rooted in the psychological addiction to risk he had developed as a side effect of piloting FLAG's efforts, of constantly facing danger, and reducing hazards in his mind to the realm of the mundane.

Adrenalin rushed into his bloodstream, spiking his nerves.

A thread of pain planted itself just above his left eye as he drove to meet Goliath head-on, now running at a hundred miles per hour.

'Give me the web safety harness,' said Michael, keeping his eyes on the road. The shoulder straps dropped obligingly down from the cabin ceiling.

Goliath gave a teeth-jarring blast on its airhorn, barrelling onward like a charging buffalo against a black mouse.

'Michael, the odds of our being victorious in a head-on confrontation with a vehicle that size, and featuring the Bonded Molecular Shell, I compute as being next to nothing.'

'I want Garthe to think I'm crazy enough to charge him, thinking I can win,' explained Michael, talking fast because they were eating up space. Goliath was nearly on top of them.

'*I got that impression*,' KITT said dryly. '*That you're crazy, I mean. You're exhibiting a dangerous indifference to serious risk.*'

'Never mind that,' said Michael, thinking perhaps it would be a better idea to keep his problems to himself for a change. 'He won't swerve. I want him to think we won't, either, that we think we'll somehow survive. I want you to cut hard left at the last possible second. It might cost us a fender . . . but I think we can take out his right front wheel. And that'll render Goliath academic as far as the raid on Red Bluff goes.'

'*But the odds are –*'

'Enough with the odds! You've been gambling too much lately.'

'*This plan is easy for you to concoct*,' said KITT. '*But it's* my *fender we're talking about losing here*!'

Goliath's horn gave another blast as the huge shape filled up KITT's windshield.

'Brace yourself, old buddy!' Michael yelled over the deafening report.

There was no more distance left.

Tsombe Kuna watched the spectacle with the avidity of a roman centurion attending an arena sacrifice of Christians to lions. The PAX-3 binoculars were socketed into his eyes, and the high-tech joust unfolding out there on the desert hardpack diverted even the attention of Kumenya, the Chiruwi bodyguard, disrupting the stony calm of his face with a kind of keen, predatory interest.

Perhaps the tiny car would try to outmanoeuvre the juggernaut, thought Kuna. That was the only chance for a contest. Goliath, like his Biblical namesake, undoubtedly had the brawn.

He rattled about in his canvas-backed lounge chair, alight with excitement. 'They're going to hit – !'

KITT and Goliath met, head-on.

Distance made it difficult to tell at what angle the two vehicles made impact, but the decision was clear: the sleek street machine flew into the air, shearing sideways like a fighter jet peeling out of formation, its right front fender torn away like a banana peel. It struck the ground on its left headlight and its speed carried it through a lateral series of somersaults. Its hood, ripped away, spun in the air like a giant tiddlywink and crashed to earth. KITT continued flipping over, losing parts along the way, gouging ditches in the ground. Finally, what was left of the black car flopped over onto its roof, slid another thirty yards, and came to rest, smoking, wheels turning slowly, rocking back and forth. There was no sign of life.

The Red Berets threw up a jubilant cheer, and Goliath's air horn tooted in response, a victory cry. The big truck lurched with a hiss of diesel brakes, and turned back to the test compound none the worse for wear.

Garthe jumped down from the cab and embraced Kuna, delirious with joy. 'Imagine, Tsombe! Tanks! Aircraft! All like this!' He indicated Goliath's front end. There were some white smudges on the chromed crash bumper where KITT had glanced off, but the truck was otherwise unscathed. 'Cameramen!'

Obediently, the video crew snapped to attention.

'Run back the tape. I want to see how it looked from here!'

They complied, and Garthe watched the sequence unfold, savouring the full view of KITT going into an airspin and losing pieces like a kid losing marbles. He laughed and clapped his hands together.

'This area has served its purpose, my brother,' he said, not taking his eyes off the unmoving wreck that was KITT. 'It's now time to move on, to Dry Lake.'

Tsombe nodded, obviously excited by the prospect. 'Then everything is on schedule?'

'Yes. I've had Mother set up a suite for us downtown, at the Mint.'

'You move quickly,' said Tsombe.

'A moving target is harder to hit,' replied Garthe. 'Especially when it moves unexpectedly, and in patterns that defy logic.'

'The truck, Goliath, it is to serve as weapons transport?'

Garthe nodded. 'I presume you've arranged the cargo plane for Dry Lake? Tomorrow?'

'It is on schedule. I should like to see how my own drivers fare in piloting Goliath.' As an afterthought he added, 'That is, in case something untoward should befall you.'

'No wild cards in this deck,' said Garthe. 'I'll be there and Goliath will be there, with the goods.' He picked up a field telephone, patched through the limousine radiophone, and called Elizabeth. 'Let's go into town and have a celebratory supper.'

They abandoned the smashed form of KITT where it had come to rest, with the limp body inside hanging, inert, in the harness webbing of the shoulder straps.

10

The Las Vegas branch of FLAG was a nondescript concrete-block building on South Sandhill Road, all mirrored windows and expensive landscaping. Floral cacti decorated the parking lot from wooden box planters. In an office on the second floor, April Curtis gazed forlornly out the window towards the highway leading out of town, and wondered just where the devil Michael Knight was, and what had happened to KITT.

Inside the nexus of computer terminals and monitoring equipment, KITT's long-distance operations monitor had emitted an unseemly squawk and then gone totally dead after putting KITT's location somewhere in that southern desert. The car and Michael were missing in action, and had not checked in for over two hours.

Devon re-entered the room, having gone to wash his face and hands in the upstairs lavatory. His exterior presented the usual authoritative calm and urbane detachment, but he was genuinely upset within. His last contact with Elizabeth could be creatively described as a draw, or, since they were in Vegas, a 'push'. No winners. Then Michael had insisted on haring off after Garthe, with little food or sleep. His FLAG field man was operating at less than maximum alertness, and that carried dangers. Part of the reason risk did not upset Michael while he was taking it was the realization that Devon worried enough for both of them – willingly, too.

'I still can't raise them, either on KITT's communications net, or Michael's comlink,' April told her father as he neared the console.

'Blasted boy,' muttered Devon. 'Thinks he's a Bedouin or some desert rat.'

From the doorway a female voice said, 'They told me downstairs that I could find Devon Miles up here.' The last word of the question curled upward, as though the statement was a question.

Devon stiffened. For a split second he thought Elizabeth had tracked him to the FLAG office for another round in their apparently endless thrust-and-parry relationship. When he saw it wasn't Elizabeth, he relaxed a notch, and then his wariness returned when he realized that it was Rita Wilcox speaking.

Gone was the expensive dunnage that made her look like a cross between an expensive harlot and a poor little rich girl. She wore a lightweight Western shirt with a colourful yoke, tight jeans and high-heeled boots. Her eyes were once again the bright, inquisitive blue Michael had noticed during his first visit to the blackjack table at Caesar's, and her hair was unbridled and freshly washed . . . as though she had slipped out of her role as Garthe Bishop's mistress like a snake shedding a skin.

'I set him up,' she said, in a tone of admission. 'I should have been able to read Garthe more clearly than I did. I should have known that *he* had known, all along. He has a weird kind of sixth sense about getting double-crossed, almost like he's not quite human, you know what I mean?'

'Michael believed you and acted on your information in good faith,' said Devon. 'You're not responsible for Garthe's actions. We don't even really know if Michael is in some kind of jeopardy, or whether he's just gone incommunicado.' This last was a frequent gambit of Michael's – often the folks at FLAG had no idea what he was doing until after his mission was accomplished. Michael was, after all, the maverick of the team.

Yes, thought Devon, Michael vanished a lot. But never to the accompaniment of KITT's long-distance operations monitor dropping dead.

'Are we going to sit around here wondering and waiting all week?' April said, irritated. She also envied Rita her casual clothes; in her Knight Industries work jumper, she felt less attractive than their visitor.

'Of course not,' said Devon. 'I've decided to fly to SAC Headquarters this afternoon and confront General Maddux in person. He won't admit the Red Bluff missile dump even exists – and it'll be impossible to requisition help to stop a nonexistent weapons cache from being robbed. There is the disconcerting possibility that since the SHOR-ATTAC missiles are quite deliberately kept secret from the public-at-large, the government won't even investigate the theft, if Garthe pulls it off. I'm going to go and try to prevent that, not because I think Garthe will succeed, but because it's foolish not to prepare for the worst.'

'Load your gun with big bullets,' nodded Rita, 'to ensure you never have to shoot the gun.'

'Precisely.'

'The semi is ready to roll on any signal, or on your order,' April told Devon. She never let their common blood interfere with the businesslike execution of FLAG's day-to-day protocol.

'Good.' Turning to Rita, he said, 'You'll stay with us, of course?'

'Garthe might get suspicious if I don't turn up back at the hotel suite,' said Rita. 'He knows Michael Knight was laying for him, but I don't think he knows I was the one who suggested the stakeout.' She knew her duty, and accepted the responsibility of the role she'd chosen. 'I just wanted to let you guys know I really am on your side, and that if there's any way I can help Michael, to just let me know.'

This neatly ignored the fact that her 'help' had possibly led to Michael's demise in the desert. Instead of pounding that sore point into the ground, Devon reverted to his customary diplomatic tact: 'Michael is perfectly capable of assessing the risks in a field-operative situation,' he said. 'You shouldn't assume it's your fault, Rita – you've taken quite a few risks yourself, being in such close orbit around Garthe, who is – as I'm sure you've noticed – not quite sane.'

She bowed her head. She had lived through Garthe's rages, been to bed with him, and been touched by the boiling anger that seemed to seethe from his pores. Oh yeah, she thought, I've noticed, all right.

'Call me if Michael turns up,' she said. 'Phone Caesar's and ask for Ting. He's trustworthy. And I'll get the message right away.' With that, she turned and left.

'I've got to get going, too,' said Devon. 'Do you want to take the truck out on the road, or wait here in hopes of some word from Michael?'

April simply turned back to the console screen, and after a moment Devon left.

The hoofbeats of approaching consciousness were not welcome in Michael Knight's head, because they were the harbingers of pain. Pain verified that he was alive, but the assertion did not please him as aches and throbs began to settle into place.

Flaring agony in his left arm. Head full of sharp needles; fiery pain.

Legs in a tangle. Hard to breathe. A stench his mind took a moment to identify - burning circuitry, the acrid, ozone odour of melted insulation.

Michael fancied he could hear his own blood dripping out of him. No, it had to be some fluid from the car...

He took a chance on opening one eye to the world. As it turned out, only one eye worked - the left one was filled up with stinging blood.

The world was upside down, and Michael saw it through a milky web, as though he had been trapped and poisoned by a giant spider. Or perhaps a snake - his ears registered a sinister hissing.

His vision focused and he saw he was staring out through KITT's windscreen. He had never seen a hunk of the supposedly unbreakable Knight Industries plexiglass broken before, but the spiderweb he had fancied he saw a moment before was the shatter-pattern of white cracks in the front window. The hiss was a hydraulic leakage somewhere in the rear of the vehicle; KITT's equivalent of the blood Michael was losing even as he awakened.

The world was still upside-down. Pressure on his shoulders told Michael he was on his back, head down, his feet above him somewhere, one knee mashed against the steering column, one arm painfully trapped in the safety harness webbing. It pulsed dully, as though broken.

'KITT?' He regretted speaking. He had bitten his lower lip almost clear through, chipping his teeth together, when Goliath half-rammed them into dreamland.

Light played erratically across the display on the vox-box, followed by unintelligible, sputtering static.

'KITT?' He fought to form words. 'Come on, old buddy, speak to me.'

A tendril of grey electrical smoke curled up from somewhere beneath Michael's head. It was not constant, so he did not worry about it.

'*Micha-l . . .*'

The change in KITT's simulated voice was shocking. It was like a weak radio broadcast through storm clouds, dropping in and out. Pieces of words were missing. '*I'm afra-d we zigg-d wh-n we sho-ld have zagged, Micha-l.*'

Something beneath the Super Dash fizzed angrily, then underwent electronic psychosis, freaking out in a spray of hot white sparks.

'*My transm-tter,*' KITT said. '*R-diotelephone conta-t is no longer p-ssible.*'

'KITT, can you spring the driver's side door? I'm stuck in here.'

'*I'll try.*'

Michael heard the relay clicking ineffectually inside the door's locking mechanism. He put his free foot against the door from the inside and pushed. The door creaked open with a trash-compacter grating, the sound of bending aluminium and breaking plastic.

His legs were asleep, due to his inverted position. He

managed an awkward sort of reverse somersault, which spilled him in a sprawl on the arid dirt after the shoulder harnesses were automatically released. His vision swam when he hit the ground.

KITT's right wheel well loomed above him. It had been compressed so that it chomped into the flat-proof foam tyre like the jaws of a huge clamp. KITT's hood lay on the ground fifty yards away. The upside-down car listed towards Michael due to the crumpled roof.

He struggled to his knees, and immediately a wave of nausea knocked him back on his face in the sand.

KITT's trunk had sprung open on landing; components and equipment were scattered around the rear of the car. Michael crawled back into the cabin on his belly and retrieved the first-aid kit from the back seat, or, more properly, the roof above the back seat. He gobbled a handful of painkillers.

'KITT? I'm going to get the gas jack and try to turn you back over.'

'*Splend-d idea. C-n you move?*'

'Enough to set this thing off,' he asserted, while another wave of pain tried to knock him down.

The gas jack was a tripod-mounted leverage device. Properly aimed, it would flip KITT right-side-up like a turtle. Michael pointed the device, touched the switch, and watched the steel legs of the tripod dig into the ground as it got a grip and shoved. KITT began to creak onto his left side.

'*This is undignif-ed,*' KITT moaned.

Michael's voice was hoarse. 'Can you give me a damage report?'

'*My turbine is out,*' the machine responded. '*Fuel syst-m damaged. Visu-l display syst-ms at one-quart-r power. And you don't look so gre-t, yourself.*'

'Forget about me. How about getting us out of here?'

'*Micha-l, my vital signs monit-r still functions, and it informs me th-t you are in urgent ne-d of medic-l assistance. We have to get you to a doct-r.*'

'Then we have to get you running,' Michael said. 'Because

I sure don't see any taxis or ambulances around here waiting for customers.'

The chemicals began to kick into Michael's metabolism, dulling the pain but not eliminating it entirely. He watched KITT drop down onto all four wheels with a thump, then disengaged the gas jack and burrowed into the glove compartment.

'I sure hope the printed schematic is still in here,' he said.

'*I nev-r leave home witho-t it*,' KITT said.

He found the folded set of blueprints. Since most of the blades on KITT's power turbine were shot, he'd have to hook up the ramjet power unit. He'd done it once at the Knight Industries lab, but never in the field, and now he regretted not paying more attention while he had been going through the motions of repair and maintenance. He dearly wished April was present, to work her mechanical miracles on KITT. This time, they were truly alone.

He had a sudden inspiration, and delved back into the glovebox compartment. Checking beneath the Super Dash, he discovered a number of simple blown fuses, and these he replaced to bring back most of KITT's voice – he was going to need KITT's help, if they were to persevere.

'*That feels much better*,' noted KITT. '*Almost normal*.' The static in his voice remained as a rude reminder that all was not well, at least, not yet.

'We have to vent the ramjet in order to get power,' Michael said distractedly. 'Your exhaust system can't handle the kind of temperatures this thing produces.'

'*I've never had this experience before*,' said KITT. '*Feeling so vulnerable, I mean. And mortal*.'

Michael stopped and leaned on the car to catch a breath. His left arm stung with pain again; he thought he could feel his bones grinding together whenever he shifted it. 'Getting a taste of your own mortality, eh?'

'*I don't like it*,' the machine said with simple finality.

'Me, neither. But we're quite a piece from home, old pal, and we're gonna have to take our chances getting back. Let's see if I can fit this thing into your engine configuration.'

'But what about you, Michael? Are you . . . intact *enough to install the needed equipment?'*

Michael decided to keep his catalogue of pains and injuries to himself. His arm was a purgatory just to move, his vision kept swimming in and out of focus, his legs were unsure, unsteady even on the level ground, and his head pounded with pain like an abscessed tooth. His nose bleed, his cuts and scrapes, all seemed superficial, but he was worried there might be some internal damage he or KITT could not pinpoint.

'I'll live,' he said at last, and grimly commenced linking up the ramjet unit, pausing only to wipe the blood from his eyes, and thinking more and more of Garthe Bishop.

Devon detested governmental waste, and was familiar with the rule of thumb that stated a normal fifty-cent lead pencil traditionally cost the Army something in the neighbourhood of ten dollars and fifty cents of taxpayers' money.

General Thaddeus Maximillian Maddux's receiving room and office were spartan, by Defence Department standards at least. They were still overdone. After repeating his urgent purpose to half a dozen guards and four secretaries, Devon found himself waiting for Maddux to return from a late lunch.

In the time Devon wasted waiting, Michael might have died a thousand times.

At last, a prim fortyish secretary smiled artificially and told Devon he would be received. It seemed fitting that Maddux did not stoop to re-entering the building through his own office complex; obviously he had a private entrance.

Or he had been holed up in his office away from prying eyes, instructing his secretaries to lie on his behalf because he had known Devon's purpose all along, and felt guilty about covering up the existence of Red Bluff.

Once he found himself facing the inevitable wood-panelled walls and array of expensive flags flanking the desk, Devon watched Maddux begin obfuscating before the Knight Industries man could even open his mouth. Maddux was endomorphic but trim, a fit fifty-eight or so. His pressed uniform fit him like a plastic glove. They did not shake hands.

'Good to see you again, Devon,' he said, with a heartiness that was conspicuously overdone. 'I'm glad I've got this opportunity to clarify my position in person. I've given your request all due consideration, but of course, you must realize that a phone call to the President would only put *my* butt in a very big sling, since you cannot prove any of your allegations.'

'It's very simple,' said Devon. 'Either you confront reality or not. Red Bluff is going to be attacked tomorrow whether you admit its existence or not. You're dealing with the kind of nuclear terrorism that our current President is constantly telling us he is prepared to squash. Well, here's his chance to put down the raid and win himself a few votes at re-election time.'

'My hands are tied, Devon. I need proof of the impending raid. Attack plans. Terrorists with known dossiers. Otherwise, all I have is your word . . . and all *you* have is the word of your agent, Michael Knight. It has more holes than a sponge.'

Devon realized he should have known anyone's word would not be sufficient incentive for Maddux to act. He would protest that he had higher-ups to answer to, that he could not accept the responsibility, that Devon was being paranoid . . . everything, in fact, except any practical action. It reminded Devon why Wilton Knight had created FLAG in the first place.

Maddux used Devon's hesitation to plough further, establishing his case: 'Think, man, for a moment. A supercar formula. African revolutionaries. Good and evil twins. Double-dealing in Las Vegas. Good God, you don't want Strategic Air Command – you want Twentieth Century-Fox! When you spoke of an international crisis, I agreed to give you a fair hearing. But consider this: Even if somebody had the resources to go after something like Red Bluff, it would be like Goldfinger going after Fort Knox.'

'Then you admit Red Bluff exists?'

Maddux grinned. 'I admit a mountain called Red Bluff exists. I didn't say anything about nuclear missiles.'

Devon sighed; the sound of a man being suffocated by red tape and 'no comment'.

'Off the record,' Maddux said, 'it doesn't matter anyway. Surely you realize the purpose of an outdated SHOR-ATTAC dump... that is, if one existed.'

Wearily, Devon said, 'Why don't you enlighten me?'

'It's perfectly obvious,' Maddux said with a highfalutin' air that was a bit maddening. 'The government would only hold back antiquated nuclear weapons in stockpile if it planned to sell those weapons to Third World countries desiring some kind of minor-league nuclear capability.'

Devon saw the light. 'Of course. Such countries couldn't use short-range weapons to become the sort of power the United States would have to worry about... we've got the big guns, so it doesn't matter if we give away the slingshots. On the other hand, a group of squabbling little countries might wipe each other out with such weapons... and all a major country would have to do is stroll in and claim the wasteland that is left. Or better yet, some of those tiny countries might get angry and lob a couple of SHOR-ATTACS at the USSR the next time it tries to invade. The Soviet Union is a lot closer than the United States.'

Maddux pursed his lips and nodded gravely. 'So, if an imaginary terrorist group stole some imaginary missiles and took them to the Third World *for* us, well, that relieves the United States of a great deal of culpability, now, doesn't it?'

'The cash value of the missiles would be nothing next to the propaganda value of having clean hands,' Devon saw. He visualized the President's hotline phone call to the Kremlin: *Oh, but WE didn't do anything, comrade, it was those nasty old terrorists...*

The phone on Maddux's desk buzzed, and the general lifted the receiver. 'Yes? Who? Oh yes –' Cupping the receiver, he said, 'Devon? I've been waiting for this call. Do you mind?'

Disgusted, Devon kept a civil face. 'Of course not.' Without a farewell he turned and backtracked to the outer office.

When the door clicked shut, Maddux resumed speaking into the phone. 'No, darling, of course I don't mind you calling me here. I've missed you terribly. No, you're not interrupting anything; I just disposed of some extra-curricular business, that's all. I think dinner this evening would be lovely, yes. Yes. Let's make it late, say eight-ish? Fine. I'll see you then.'

A look of pleasure crossed his face as he signed off. 'Yes. Me, too. I'll see you this evening, Elizabeth.'

11

The commercial warehouse facility, with its faded sign still reading CORSICAN EXTENDABLES LTD., had sat totally empty for over a year. The renters had not required it until now.

Most of the building was still steeped in the dust of disuse, but just inside the central loading bay there was a wasp-buzzing of calculated activity. Technicians tended to the gleaming hulk of Goliath under work-lights. The scratches that were the only visible evidence of KITT's recent demise had been neatly erased from the crash bumpers.

Garthe could not keep from walking around the truck, admiring it openly, and basking in his own self-satisfaction. Tsombe Kuna had been pleased, and that pleased Garthe... but something uncomfortable remained unspoken between the two unlikely allies, and Garthe, in his insistent, probing way, wanted to know what it was.

'A miracle of American technology,' Kuna said of the truck. 'This development will be of great consequence to the Pan-African Liberation Movement. The implications of this demonstration could change the face of the entire continent of Africa – and if Africa changes, the world will change, is it not so?' He spread his broad hands as if the alteration of world history was obvious to anyone possessing a brain.

Garthe attempted to dismiss the two looming Red Berets behind Kuna with a withering glance, but they stood fast and primed to jump, rather like Dobermanns, Garthe thought – essentially stupid animals good for a limited range of use. 'If Goliath is anyone's miracle, Tsombe,' he said in a quiet hiss, 'it's mine.'

Tsombe surprised him by laughing his deep-register laugh.

He folded his arms within his loud tribal robes. 'Of course it is, my brother,' he said with a hint of contempt. 'Why, you could walk across the Boulder Dam reservoir if necessary, and change tap water into burgundy, and call the thunder down from the skies to change the land. Of course.'

Garthe glared, then turned to stomp off. Tsombe put out a hand to stay him.

'Linger for a moment, my brother,' he said, and the command to stay was clear. 'We must discuss a matter of some importance. Having a rather substantial investment in this enterprise, being partners as it were, I think you should take an interest in certain developments that disturb me.'

Garthe gritted his teeth, suppressing an urge to lash out and kill Kuna instantly by breaking the bridge of the broad African nose with the heel of his hand, driving bone splinters into the brain and causing fast death. 'Such developments as –?' he said pleasantly.

'Elizabeth Bishop informs me that there is a matter of a personal vendetta between you and the driver of the black car you destroyed this afternoon.'

Garthe suppressed his rage behind an unmoving mask of emotionlessness. His mother had dared to speak to Kuna without telling him – that was not a good omen. He remembered the incidents following the demonstration, after he had returned to the Mint suite in downtown Vegas . . .

'What a brash, stupid thing to do,' Elizabeth had chided him. 'You might have blown the whole plan – over a year of work – countless thousands spent. And you might have flushed it all this afternoon just to satisfy your petty, juvenile need for revenge!'

'Nothing will go wrong,' he asserted, concentrating on a celebratory glass of champagne gone suddenly sour.

'You should have killed Michael Knight when the opportunity presented itself,' she said sternly.

'I have plans, yet, for Michael Knight.' That was it – contemplation of what he wished to do to his goody-goody twin brought his spirits back up. 'Today was just a taste from a whole rancid banquet I've planned for him. Now we let the fear build awhile, and engulf him.'

'Wrong,' snapped Elizabeth. 'There is only one plan, and by not applying your full attention to it, you're going to get us all chucked in the slammer because of your rivalry with Michael bloody Knight! I have a say in this operation, and I won't permit it!' Then, with unexpected cheek, she turned and slapped the glass from Garthe's hand. Bubbly flew into the air. The glass bounced on the carpet and did not break.

Elizabeth uttered a short little gasp, because Garthe had seized her wrist and was twisting it painfully, his face still expressionless.

'Dear Mother,' he said, squeezing the nerve pressure point, producing exquisite pain. 'I'm not your little boy anymore. I do what I please, when I please.'

'You're hurting my arm . . .' The blood left her face.

'You can stand it,' he said. 'Pretend you're playing musical beds with another of our patsies. That should ease the hurt. But know this – it pleases me to keep Michael Knight alive for the moment, whether you like it or not, for reasons purely my own. Now, would you please pour me another glass of champagne, darling Mother?'

'Not on your life,' she gasped.

He twisted savagely and Elizabeth yelped. 'Reconsider, why don't you? You'll find it difficult to seduce our ageing functionaries with a broken arm.'

'All . . . all right . . .' She had backed down again, realising that without warning, Garthe could become homicidal to get whatever he desired. She massaged her released wrist for a second, moved to the bar, poured the champagne . . . and threw it in his face.

He flinched but did not strike her. Then he shook his head, and a low laugh escaped him. 'Two like coins, eh, Mother?' With wine running down his face and off his chin, he calmly prepared a cracker of caviar for himself. He offered it to Elizabeth first. 'Why don't you have some? It's Beluga. It's good.'

Elizabeth left the room in a huff, and Garthe gulped down the cracker, smirking, sweating champagne.

That had been only an hour or two before. Now Tsombe Kuna was giving him the same agony over Michael Knight.

Kuna stared at him levelly. 'So why did you not kill this Michael Knight? You had ample opportunity. To avoid the chance for revenge is not sound battle strategy.'

'I shall,' Garthe said, controlled. 'Soon.'

'But you had your chance, and did not,' Kuna emphasized. 'So much depends on your success in the next twenty-four hours. I should hate to think you'd fail so obviously in carrying out *our* plan.'

Garthe concentrated on Kuna while the guards sensed danger in the air and stiffened, doglike. 'No one tells me how to proceed with Red Bluff,' he said. 'Not you. Not my redoubtable Mother. You'll get what you want. Just remember you'd still be running around the sedge in a wicker jockstrap, dodging spears, if it wasn't for me.'

Kuna gave him a reptilian smile. 'And without me, my *brother*, you would today be a maggot-ridden corpse in the bone-disposal pit at the Tongo M'Kimbe death camp.' He waited a beat, then added, 'So, we are mutually indebted. With luck, we shall continue our long and fruitful relationship. But on this matter of vendetta – it is disturbing. Why not avoid it? I have several excellent drivers among my staff; I'm sure they could pilot Goliath. You need not risk yourself during the Red Bluff raid.'

'Nowhere am I safer than in Goliath.'

'If you prove unreliable again, my brother, my concerns will not be so broadly for your safety.'

'Don't bother with threats, Tsombe,' he said, his own counter-threat implicit. 'Not at this stage.'

'I never threaten, brother. I merely remind you of your obligations.'

'Yeah, right.' Garthe was beginning to think that perhaps Kuna could be somehow erased from the plan . . . after the raid, of course. Replaced with someone more agreeable.

With a swish of robes, Kuna returned to his air-conditioned limousine.

When Devon returned to the Las Vegas headquarters of the Foundation, he found April still sitting hopefully in front of the information terminal. He had called three times during his trip back, and there had been no word on Michael's fate. He really did not expect good news.

'Nothing yet,' she said listlessly. 'How'd it go with General Maddux?'

'Nothing *went*,' said Devon with disappointment and frustration. 'Without signed affadavits from Garthe Bishop putting down his plan in detail, Maddux won't even grant an audience . . . and the government's not truly interested in stopping him, anyway.'

'That's why *we're* here,' April said, trying to cheer him up. 'There are areas not covered by laws, or governments, or armies . . . despite what we call ourselves.'

'I suppose you're right. It all just seems so . . . so futile.'

'What?'

'To think that Michael may have died out there; given his life in vain.'

Fear jumped into her eyes. 'I don't want to think about that,' she said quietly.

'I want to be cremated,' came a voice from the doorway. 'I want April to scatter white rose petals all over wherever you dump my ashes.'

They turned and saw Michael, leaning heavily against the doorjamb, his clothing torn, his face blotched with dirt and streaks of blood. They called out his name simultaneously, he fell on his face, and that was the last thing he remembered for a while.

Somebody was saying 'Goliath' over and over as Michael woke up. The name reverberated inside his skull, causing pain, more of which he did not need since he was full to the brim already – enough so that coming back to consciousness was repugnant to him.

Hardness. His left arm was bound up in a sling of white hospital-issue cloth.

'Hello?' he said, his voice ragged. Other voices responded.

'– seems to be coming round –'

'– whopping load of painkillers in him –'

'– he sound? Internally, I mean?'

For a moment he was reminded of KITT's malfunctioning vox-box, spewing out sentence fragments. April was here; so was Devon. He opened one eye and saw them, then the other eye. Two doctors loomed over him, one male, one female.

'Welcome back to the land of the living,' said the woman.

Across town, Garthe was dallying with Rita Wilcox, having just endured the ugly scenes with Tsombe Kuna and Elizabeth. Elizabeth was dressing for her dinner date with General Maddux. Kuna was sequestered inside a huge Winnebago he had purchased between arguments with Garthe, finalizing plans for the next day's raid. Red Berets surrounded the RV like ants guarding an anthill.

'Where's KITT?' Michael said to no one in particular.

'Diagnostic bay,' said April. 'He's in worse shape than you, and that's going a fair piece.'

He grimaced, then continued: 'How soon can he roll?'

April considered telling him it was impossible, but knew he'd object. 'Five hours,' she said. 'But it'll take you longer just to be able to focus your vision.'

'The hell it will,' said Michael. 'I've concocted a little plan of my own. Garthe is going to get a taste of his own therapy *tonight*.'

'Now, just a moment,' said Devon. 'You're in here as a result of your last rash action. Are you so eager to repeat the experience? KITT told us all about the confrontation with Goliath, and it seems obvious to us that Goliath is the means by which Garthe and Tsombe Kuna intend to break into Red Bluff.'

'I've got to be there when he does,' said Michael. 'Don't you see? It's all in his plan – otherwise, I'd be drawing flies in the desert right now.'

'I don't follow,' said April.

'Garthe pulped me and KITT to flaunt his superiority. He's hung up, idealogically, on the fact that I "took his place" as far as Wilton Knight was concerned. He wants me to see him victorious at Red Bluff *despite* my attempts to stop him – to prove he was the better man all along. You see? I can't *not* show up.'

'Very elegant reasoning, Micahel,' said Devon. 'But how does it help us?'

'My own plan,' Michael said from the bed. 'Garthe can't stand the thought of losing to me, in any way, shape, or form. I've got a little psychological attack thought up, but I'm going to need KITT to do it, and that's why we've both got to be mobile by nightfall.'

Devon looked immediately to the physicians. 'Can he stand any action tonight?'

'I'd advise against it. He needs bed rest.'

'Believe me,' said Michael, 'there's nothing I'd love more. But you know that old saw about how "the impossible takes us a little bit longer –"?'

'I understand,' said the male doctor. 'We have stimulants that can make you functional – but you have to promise to rest on the other end.'

'Just get me through tomorrow.'

The doctors and Devon exchanged uneasy looks. Michael guiltily speculated on just how destroyed he must look, there in bed, taped together.

April was already on her way out the door. 'If you're going to pump him full of drugs and shove him out the door, I've got to get to work on KITT pronto . . . so they both don't get killed.' There was a strong hint of disapproval in her tone, and Devon suspected his daughter had become as fond of Michael as she was of KITT. Some things could not be helped.

'Just leave everything to me tonight,' Michael croaked. Nobody appeared convinced.

12

Garthe straightened his bow tie and slipped into his boots. His tuxedo fairly shimmered. He winked at himself in the full length mirror, then slanted his gaze so that he could see Rita behind him, still dressing.

'Something?' he said.

She wobbled on one heel, putting on the other shoe. 'What do you mean?'

'Something the matter? You seemed distracted. I wouldn't want our special little times together to become ordinary, humdrum, you know?'

'No,' she lied. 'I think I strained a tendon while I was exercising earlier. It hurts when I move my leg a certain way, that's all.'

He moved to her, grabbed her by the shoulders, and pulled her close for a kiss. She submitted. His snake-like gaze projected past her shoulder as he said, 'There's no one else but me, is there, Rita darling?' It was the same haunting tone with which he'd spoken to his mother, earlier, while threatening her.

'Of course not,' she said robotically. It was a question she answered often. 'How could there be?'

'There couldn't,' he smiled, and released her, since she had performed as ordered. 'Be sure you bring me luck this evening. I despise losing.'

'I'll be there if I can ever get my other shoe on. Ouch!' Finally, in deference to the imaginary strained tendon, she sat on the bed to don her footwear.

As offhandedly as possible, as he walked towards the bathroom, Garthe tossed back over his shoulder: 'Oh, by the way, I'm awfully sorry about your brother.'

Rita froze. 'What about Ron?'

'You mean you haven't heard?' He shrugged, as with a childish perplexity. 'A geological survey crew found his . . . er, *remains* in the desert about ten miles east of Leadwater. They say he died of exposure.'

He relished the expression on her face, the way it crumpled at the news. Silly twit, he thought. He already suspected her of consorting with Michael Knight, and for that little offence, she would soon join her dead, dumb brother. But that entertainment was for later.

'I'll expect you downstairs in the casino in fifteen minutes,' he said. She did not respond. He thought he heard a sob leak out of the bedroom, but that did not matter. Nothing did, to him, except the straight fall of his seams and the razor sharpness of his pleats. Then he grabbed the diamond-topped ebony cane. In all his sartorial splendour, he was ready to gamble.

'You mean cheating,' KITT admonished Michael. *'When you speak of beating Garthe at his own game, you mean you intend to use me to help you cheat.'*

Dressed in formal evening wear – including a black silk sling for his damaged arm – Michael drove to the MGM Grand, across the street from Caesar's. The Grand was where he would find Garthe tonight, and work the plan he had referred to so obliquely in the hospital.

'It's not exactly cheating,' Michael hemmed and hawed.

'Just like when we make haste somewhere, it's "not exactly" speeding?'

'Something like that. We're the good guys.'

'So we can break the law with impunity? Like peeking at my hands in computer blackjack?'

'I never –!'

'You owe me four hundred and thirteen dollars regardless.'

Michael skipped over it as the night-lights of the Strip whizzed by outside his window. 'Besides, Garthe's passion is for craps, not blackjack.'

'An aptly named game,' said KITT, *'considering its outrageous odds system.'*

'But it's more a game of pure chance than a lot of other casino games. You know some of these joints gross a million bucks a day and they still can't operate in the black?'

They turned into the lot of the bronze-fronted MGM Grand Hotel, which squatted on the Strip like some awesome, high-tech Aztec pyramid.

'I don't know if I'm ready for this, Michael,' KITT said skittishly. *'Remember the test this afternoon.'*

Michael remembered. He had limped into KITT's diagnostic bay to see his mechanical partner getting a new fender, a new hood . . . and some other strange items that did not come under the heading of custom options. Most of the hideous cosmetic damage wrought by sideswiping Goliath had been repaired. The ramjet unit was back in the trunk, where Michael preferred it to be. KITT had been undergoing turbine tests and electrical adjustments. April had been sweating away on her 'impossible' schedule, yet nevertheless had made two interesting additions.

'I pulled the resonating laser out of mothballs,' she announced.

'That thing we used last year to try and knock KARR out of commission?' Michael said. 'As I recall, it didn't work worth beans.'

'This is an improvement over the one Bonnie Barstow installed in KITT,' she said, 'which, from my reading of the data fetch on that mission, you guys used improperly anyway. This is more idiot-proof.'

'Thanks,' he said, rolling his eyes.

'No, what I mean is, for one thing, targeting is automatic, zeroed-in through KITT's scanner instead of eyeline contact. If Goliath has a weak spot, you can punch a hole in it with the laser. Also, my revamped version is good for more than a single shot.'

'I wish we'd had it yesterday,' KITT lamented, his prosthetic voice normal now. *'Or maybe one of those nuclear*

SHOR-ATTAC missiles to shoot through the windscreen of that black behemoth.'

'Ah, for that, we have this,' she said, producing a cigarette-pack-sized metal box which she handed to Michael.

'The concussion cap?' said Michael.

'Just as you ordered, sir,' she smiled. 'Plant this in Goliath's wheel well, and I guarantee the wheel will go flying when you punch the red button... although I don't know how you intend to get that close to it.'

'Part of my plan,' he said enigmatically. 'Tip-top secret.'

'It's keyed through an LED timer I've installed below the vital signs monitor. You understand how to fire it up?'

Michael bent – painfully – and peered into KITT's cabin. The control board was about the dimensions of a credit card calculator. 'Yeah. No problem.'

'Okay,' April said, briskly retrieving another component. 'Item number three – the scientific name would really blow your mind, so let's just skip it and call it the Pusher. It works with sonics, moves small objects with ultra-high frequency sound. Given the composition of the dice cubes they use at the MGM Grand, you should be okay. But this still needs calibrating...'

'Can I see it work?'

She shrugged. 'As far as it does now.' She took an ashtray from one of the wall-mounted workbenches and placed it upside-down on the table. 'We're close enough – that is, KITT is close enough – to move a larger object than a dice cube. But for the kind of range you want I needed to install a power booster as well.'

'It's a little crowded in here,' KITT said.

April pressed a button. Michael felt something high-pitched and airy knife through his head, and the ashtray flipped over by itself.

Then it exploded, spraying hot fragments of glass all over the narrow diagnostic bay.

Michael took his hand down from his eyes. 'Still needs a bit of adjustment, eh?'

She sighed. 'You ask for a lot. I'm doing my best.'

He put his injured hands on her shoulders to reassure her. 'I know. You're the expert, not me. This stuff is terrific. Just get the bugs out by six o'clock, could you?'

'Go get me a burger and some onion rings and you've got a deal.'

'Lady, I'll buy you lobster on Fisherman's Wharf if you pull this off . . . and if I survive the next twenty-four hours without falling apart like a demolition derby jalopy.'

'I resent that remark,' interjected KITT.

He had tried to leave her smiling, and now, loaded for bear, he was about to face down Garthe, personality against personality, and now, technology versus technology. He was prepared to play dirty; he'd been mashed, KITT had been trashed, Devon had been poisoned . . .

'No more Mister Nice Guy,' he muttered as he parked in the MGM Grand lot. 'You're keyed through the comlink, KITT. I may make a comment or two but don't respond directly – casino security take a dim view of transmitting devices, if you get what I mean.

'Absolutely. Good luck, Michael.'

'Tonight I don't want luck to have anything to do with it,' he said. Straightening his lapels, he made for the casino, his limp hardly noticeable.

Garthe watched the croupier's rake push another two thousand dollars in chips into his pile, knocking down the neat stacks into an expensive mess.

'Your dice, Mr Bishop,' said the stick man, pushing the heavy, ivory-coloured casino cubes towards Garthe. He weighed them in his palm.

A stocky, crewcut man leaned into the crowd surrounding the boat-sized crap table and whispered to Garthe: 'Rita Wilcox just left the Mint. Want her followed?'

A faint smile touched the corners of Garthe's lips. 'No, Cody, not for now. Let's permit Miss Wilcox to believe she has freedom. When we leave for Red Bluff, in the morning, and after I've finished with her, let's see she joins her beloved brother Ron, hm?'

'Very good.' The operative vanished into the crush of gamblers.

Garthe shoved a bet in excess of five thousand dollars out onto the baize, and rattled the cubes in his left hand. It stroked his ego to watch most of the fish around the table betting with him . . . until his eyes crossed a pile of new chips sitting on the DON'T PASS line. His eyes sized up the stacks and totalled five thousand, the same as his own bet. Then his eyes continued upward . . . coming to rest on Michael Knight's gaze.

Garthe remained expressionless. 'We have a man here who enjoys losing,' he said, and several gamblers closest to him laughed in support.

'Only to losers,' Michael replied across the width of the table, and an icy chill descended over the gaiety of the scene. 'You going to gab, hot stick . . . or roll?'

Garthe snorted and hurled the dice against the far corner of the table. Nobody noticed one of the cubes jig crazily under the influence of the Pusher device April had installed in KITT. Instead of landing on a calculated seven, the dice came up snake eyes after dancing around a moment.

'Snake eyes, the loser,' droned the stick man, raking away Garthe's pile and adding it to Michael's.

'Thanks a bunch, snake eyes,' Michael said pointedly. He was interrupted by a voice from behind him.

'Hey, ace, how's it goin'? See you're as lucky as ever.'

Michael turned and saw the nervous gambler he had first seen playing Rita Wilcox's blackjack table, then later at Caesar's playing unknowingly against the same woman and getting cleaned out. 'Just what is your name, anyway?' he said.

'Plimpton. Abe.' He extended a sweaty palm for Michael to shake.

'Join the slaughter, Plimpton – I'm going to take this ugly dude on the other side of the table for every farthing he has.'

'Love to, ace, but can't. I'm as broke as an egg on a Tilt 'n Whirl.'

Michael flipped him a black-and-yellow bumblebee chip worth a hundred dollars. 'Grubstake, Plimpton, my man.'

Plimpton snatched the chip out of the air, shouldered himself a place among the gamblers, and slapped his money down in support of Michael. Several others, sticking with the cash flow, joined him.

The stick man slid the dice across to Michael, who picked them up and agitated them briefly. More due to skill than KITT's ultrasonic interference, he tossed a perfect seven, and there was a delicious moment of nervy anticipation as he thought his recklessness might lose the show.

More chips were shovelled towards him. Garthe glared and continued betting against him.

'Seven,' Michael whispered to himself. After a moment of thought, he pushed his $20,000 over to the COME line. Garthe instantly pushed an equivalent bet onto the DON'T COME line. 'Seven come eleven,' Michael repeated, like a mantra.

He chucked out a pair of fives . . . that jigged and became a five and a six. KITT was hanging in there, and, unobtrusively, he said to the comlink, 'Thanks, old buddy.'

'Weren't nothin'!' exclaimed Plimpton, eagerly collecting his chips and giving Michael back his hundred bucks.

Neutrally, Garthe said, 'I'd like a request our hot shooter use a new pair of dice.' He was convinced Michael's luck had to be mechanically enhanced.

'You want new dice?' Michael threw the cubes across the table at Garthe, who fumed. 'Sure. Any pair you say. Only you'd better hurry . . . because you're not going to be able to afford new dice, soon.'

Pristine new dice were produced. The stick man continued his litany; *hot shooter, place yer bets, hot stick . . .*

Michael reached into his tuxedo jacket – he and Garthe had both chosen basic black, he noticed, another mirror image – and dropped a wad of high-denomination bills onto his sprawling piles of chips. 'Fifty thousand,' he said, and everybody – including Plimpton and excepting Garthe – gasped.

'Sir,' said the stick man, according to protocol,' the table limit is twenty thousand.'

Garthe immediately glared at the man, then looked over his shoulder. The pit boss hurried over, looked from the table to Garthe, and then nodded at the stick man. 'For this player,' said the pit boss evenly, 'the limit is raised to fifty thousand. Place your bets.'

'Thank you, Ricardo,' said Garthe, relishing this display of personal power.

'Let's try one more time,' Michael said, baiting him. 'Seven come eleven.'

Several people had dropped out of play. Plimpton stuck with Michael, and Garthe matched the fifty thousand on the DON'T COME line.

Michael threw the dice for the last time.

When he did, Garthe rose from his seat and shouted, '*Snake eyes!*' as though the power of his voice could physically influence the trajectory of the dice.

And for a moment, it seemed it had. Michael and Garthe both saw the single dots come up as the dice came to rest. But as Garthe was prepared to whoop in triumph, one of the cubes flipped over to a six.

A cheer went up from half the gamblers and Plimpton slapped Michael on the back. 'Man,' he said, 'you've just won a hundred thousand dollars, ace!' He scraped his seven hundred new bucks together in his hands.

'Never bet against a winner, fireball,' Michael said to Garthe.

'In the end you will lose,' said Garthe. 'This is a pittance. In the end, you shall be mine.'

'Yeah, sure. Time to cash in, but you don't seem to have many chips left, Garthe, old boy. Say hi to your mother for me.' He winked and left Garthe stewing in anger.

Then Plimpton was slapping him on the back again.

Nervous casino guards moved around Michael as he carried his haul to the cashier's cages.

Garthe left the table moments later, in a hot huff, and did not notice one of the dice, crumbling apart like a wet sugar cube due to all the resonance set up inside of it by KITT's still-not-perfectly-calibrated Pusher device.

'You know,' said Plimpton, matching pace with the taller Michael, 'I don't even know your name.'

Michael grinned. 'Just call me the Lone Ranger.'

'I'd say the odds were certainly in our favour,' said KITT ten minutes later, once Michael was back in the cabin. They sat unmoving in the parking garage at the Grand. *'And I've pinpointed the location of Garthe Bishop's car. It's a late-model Corvette, dead black, so new it doesn't have plates yet.'*

'He didn't bring his limo, huh? Good.' Michael studied the video readout that pinpointed the car's position in the underground garage. 'Okay. He should come storming out any minute now. When he gets in his car, bollix the engine with your microwave jammers. I'll do the rest.'

'Are you certain?' said KITT apprehensively. *'You're not in top operating condition, you know.'*

'Leave it to me,' he said. 'Jeez, nobody has any faith in my ability any more.'

'Here comes Garthe.'

Michael slouched down in his bucket seat. With no audience, Garthe's true nature was a little closer to the surface. His teeth were clenched and his face a furious crimson colour. After a few heated words were exchanged, he directed Cody, his operative, into a hubcap-less Chevrolet that looked like an unmarked FBI car. As Cody drove out of the lot, Garthe seated himself in his Corvette.

'Sure wish I didn't have this damned cast on my arm,' Michael said, indicating his black silk sling.

'It's necessary. The fracture you sustained is no laughing matter.'

Garthe's engine hitched and died. He tried again. Nothing.

The Corvette made a sound much like a car with a dying alternator.

'Well,' said Michael, 'Let's see if I can tickle Garthe a little despite the cast.' Quietly, he got out of KITT. 'Pour on the microwaves. Keep his engine down.'

Garthe kicked his door open on the Corvette and popped the hood to fiddle with some of the electrical connections, cursing to himself while he did it.

Michael was three cars away, then two.

'Bloody piece of swamp garbage!' Garthe muttered, leaning further into the engine bay. 'Brand new. Pah!'

'Hey, hot stick,' Michael said quietly.

As Garthe rose at the sound of Michael's voice, Michael slammed the hood of the Corvette. Garthe's noggin bounced off the engine block and rebounded off the bottom of the hood with a pleasing *thunk-thunk*, like a basketball dropping into an empty trash can. His arms and legs sprawled.

Michael lifted the hood of the black Corvette. 'Still with us?' he said, pleasantly, as though he was a salesman showing off his top-of-the-line automobile.

Garthe grunted and tried to get his feet under him.

'Oh, good,' Michael said, the anger rising in his voice. 'Because I wanted you to see this.'

He slipped his arm, still in the cast, out of the sling and brought it down across the back of Garthe's head with all the momentum he could muster. The solid plaster cast shattered, spraying fragments all over the stark blackness of the Corvette like ungainly snowflakes. Garthe went down bonelessly, and stayed on the floor.

'Yeeeoow!' Clutching his arm, Michael danced around in a tight little circle. Fragments of the cast hung loose, and his arm was on fire with new pain.

'Michael!' came KITT's voice over the comlink. *'Are you okay? Michael?'*

He stood still long enough to respond, 'I think I broke it for real, old buddy, and it feels like I just slammed a blast-furnace door on it . . . but I feel terrific!'

Garthe, totally unconscious, remained sprawled on the floor, waiting for Michael to stop dancing.

13

Tsombe Kuna's Winnebago was more properly a fully-equipped mobile command centre incorporating essentials – like the wet bar and video bank – with sleeping quarters, short-range telecommunications rigs, and a drop-down wall panel housing a selection of loaded automatic weapons. Somewhere in the rear of the vehicle there was even a ramped compartment concealing a fuelled dirt bike, as an emergency escape contingency.

A stoic Red Beret sat at the radio console, talking in muted African dialect to the pilots of a C-14 that had taxied to a stop on the desert hardpan some hundred and fifty yards from the RV. Outside, a rainbow-hued tarpaulin in the same shades as Tsombe's beloved robes was tacked up on aluminium poles to provide shade, and several folding chairs were scattered beneath it. Tsombe enjoyed the heat of the desert; it reminded him of the African sedge.

He sipped a sickening-looking drink full of slushy ice and foliage, and cocked his ear towards the horizon. Soon all of them – Tsombe, Elizabeth, Kumenya, and the assorted Red Beret commandos – heard the sound.

Goliath was approaching from the west, its low-register thrumming and rumbling gradually filling up the valley with the sound of its power.

'As you can see, my dear Elizabeth,' Tsombe said with not a little superiority, '*my* personal driver believed in the virtues of punctuality – unlike your somewhat foolhardy son.'

Elizabeth, dressed in a chic safari suit, spun on the revolutionary leader. 'I'd watch my choice of words if I were you,' she spat. 'Like all men of great strength, Garthe has weaknesses. But they are irrelevant. You, I, these men – we serve little purpose other than to eradicate the dark patches that disrupt his light. He is destined for greatness; you and I have had to buy it, steal it, or pretend to it.'

On Tsombe's distracted, or amused, expression, she added, 'Garthe will come. On time.'

'If not, we will proceed without him.' In Garthe's absence, Tsombe was clearly relishing whatever control he could wield, and Elizabeth abruptly wondered just how loyal the Red Beret sentries were – in a crunch, would they favour Garthe or Tsombe?

'He knows,' she said, simply.

Kuna moved closer, as if sharing a confidence with her. 'Like you, Elizabeth, I have tried to reason with Garthe. He does not respond well to mere reason; he needs higher and more obscure motivations. I have tried to impress upon him the urgency of this mission, not only in terms of our immediate potential for material gain, but in terms of the long-range goals, things important to the Pan-African Liberation effort. Yet he detours himself, in order to chase fantasy enemies in the desert. Symbolic Nemeses; insidious twin versions of himself – not the sign of a stable leader of men, destined for greatness.'

Elizabeth's colour rose. 'I want to let you in on something, Tsombe, oh-great-leader to the African masses, Messiah to the waiting dispossessed. The form of this venture is daring, and it was conceived by my son – not by tiny men, with tiny minds, who live by clocks and paycheques. Garthe conceived it. I conceived it. You stand to gain a great deal from it. It was born of passion – not punctuality.'

The heat shimmer rolling off the gleaming black form of Goliath hurt the eyes. They could all see it now, barrelling towards them.

'If you're so impatient,' she continued, 'let your bloody drivers drive. Let your watchdog soldiers blast things apart with their guns, as they are trained to do. And let your dispossessed die. My son and I will triumph in the end.'

Under his breath, Tsombe said, 'Provided he gets here in

time to enjoy his great moment of glory. I don't plan to miss my own on his behalf. Remember that.'

'Save the speeches for your teeming masses,' said Elizabeth, nodding towards the south. 'I think this is Garthe, coming now.'

A black speck approached them at high speed.

Rita Wilcox had been surprised too many times in the same day.

First had come Garthe's revelation about Ron. Ron's *murder*, her mind insisted; let's call it what it really is. Then there was the evil feeling that her time as Garthe's mistress was rapidly dwindling, and she had nothing to show for it – no Ron, no revenge, no justice. Plus the vague feeling that she was being shadowed by one of Garthe's slimy operatives, possibly that creepy Jarrett character. Then there was Garthe himself to deal with; he had a habit of showing up in the suite, to spend the night, just as she'd dozed off, as though he was a character from some hideous nightmare come to haunt her bed. She felt nothing for him. Now it was impossible for her to believe that she ever had.

Michael Knight and the jolly gang at FLAG had provided a lot of fast motion, but no real movement; they were as stumped as Rita was. That thought depressed her, and hot on its heels had come that old Hemingway dictum: *Take the money and run.*

It was tempting. She could cut her losses and vanish, consider Garthe's debt to her unpayable, and just commence a new life, forgetting about Ron and his dream of starting a career as a studio musician, *their* dream of crashing the music business, she with the voice, he with the backup. Just toss it all, and move to some part of the country where such dreams wouldn't keep her awake nights.

Mechanically, moving about the expensive suite at the Flamingo, she had begun to pack her few things. All her clothing was new she noticed. Hardly a vestige of her old life – the one lived in the cinderblock apartment complex –

remained here. There was plenty of cash laying around; Garthe always left money in his wake like litter on a road. It would give her some kind of starting point. Plane fare. A grubstake, as her hapless former customer, Plimpton, might have said.

She filled a night case with clothing and a shoulder bag with money. She was almost to the door of the suite when it opened from the other side.

Garthe Bishop, dressed in natty black jeans and a silk shirt, stepped into the room and fixed her with his serpent-like gaze. Her left hand let go of the night case and it thudded on the carpeting.

'Garthe . . .' she said, barely regaining her voice, realizing she was caught red-handed in the act of lighting out. 'I . . . I thought you'd gone on to Dry Lake with the others . . .'

Then Garthe did something quite uncharacteristic. He grinned at her, and winked slyly. It wasn't Garthe Bishop's devil's-deal kind of wink; this wink was childlike, mischievious. 'Rita,' he said. 'It's me – Michael Knight.'

The shoulder bad dropped to the floor to join the night case. Then her defences went up. 'That's not funny, Garthe,' she said warily.

Then Garthe did something even more uncharacteristic – in fact, something he had never done once in his entire life. He peeled off his moustache in a single piece and held it towards her like a piece of black, hairy bait. 'It really is me,' he said.

'*Michael* –?'

'At your service.' He bowed. He held his left arm stiffly, as though it pained him to move it.

'What're you doing here?' Her head was swimming with relief and dissipated fear.

'Everyone's cleared out for their respective penthouses and suites all over town,' he said, twiddling the fake moustache between his fingers like a magician's coin trick. 'Today's the big day. If Tsombe and Elizabeth took off for Dry Lake, "Garthe" had better not disappoint them by not showing up.'

'But where's Garthe?'

'On ice. Actually, I locked him in a security room over at the Foundation's Las Vegas headquarters. Devon and April will make sure he doesn't do anything except watch daytime television until this is over.'

'What about Dry Lake?'

'It's a salt flat adjacent to Red Bluff. If the strike is to be made, it'll be made from Dry Lake. I figure Garthe planned to use Goliath – the truck – to penetrate the Red Bluff SHOR-ATTAC dump and ferry the missiles themselves back to Dry Lake, which is the closest area large and flat enough to land a cargo plane on. Then everyone flies out of the country, missiles, money, Bonded Molecular Shell formula, and all, to go change the face of the Third World.'

'You're going to go out there as Garthe?' she said, squinting at him in a peculiar fashion. 'Pose as him and mess up their plan from within?'

Michael – 'Garthe' – nodded. 'But first I have to put my moustache back on.' He moved across the the lavish suite to the nearest mirror, which was mounted beside the canopy bed.

'How did you manage the earring?' she said with a faint trace of amusement. 'If you'd just had your ear pierced you'd still be bleeding.'

'It's glued on with spirit gum,' he said, 'like the moustache. A phony post stud is glued onto the back of my earlove, and a diamond in front. Is Garthe's ebony cane anywhere around here? That's another essential prop. It wasn't inside his Corvette.'

'It's here.' She hurried to fetch it.

'You might as well come with me,' he said. 'Your presence will add verisimilitude to my act.'

Wordlessly, she decided to go with him, where a moment before she had been on the verge of cutting and running. Perhaps there was something to be salvaged from this whole mess; perhaps Ron would be avenged this afternoon.

'Besides,' Michael added, as though he'd been reading her thoughts, 'if you tried to leave your room I doubt if you'd make it out of Clark County alive. Garthe, as you may have noticed, doesn't like the concept of unfinished business.'

His moustache was cemented firmly back in place. It was difficult for Rita not to respond to the man before her with all the physical loathing she reserved for Garthe.

'I couldn't stand it any longer,' she said. 'I deluded myself that he wasn't really touching *me*, you know, the inner me . . . but he's just so creepy; it got slimier and slimier.'

'I hear that,' 'Garthe' said sympathetically.

'He's dead, you know. Ron. Garthe told me the way you'd mention an amusing commercial you'd seen on television in passing. He came in, used me, and then dropped it on me, utterly coldly.'

'I'm sorry,' said Michael.

'So am I. And the horrible thing is that I *know* he's dead now. It's not just Garthe being his usual sadistic self. Ron is dead. Bingo. The stamp of authenticity.' She looked out the window of the suite. 'I really hate this town. I'm never coming back here. If I have to drive through Montana to avoid Las Vegas, I'll do it.'

She squeezed Michael's hand, appreciative of his support. She did not say a whole lot else until they were almost to the Dry Lake location on KITT's video readout map.

'I calculate the odds of our meeting up with that meretricious mechanical mangler in excess of two to one,' KITT reported.

'You sound almost happy about it,' said Michael, while Rita watched him – or rather, 'Garthe' – talk to his own car as though it were a faithful horse.

'The odds of that hyperthyroidal highballer, that diesel dum-dum, brutalizing me again I put at four to one. Make that five!'

'We've got a shot at knocking Goliath out at least,' he said, thinking of the resonating laser April had reinstalled in KITT. It was fully charged and ready to fire. It could be used to penetrate any portion of Goliath not sheathed in the Bonded Molecular Shell. Then there was the concussion cap . . . which Michael hoped his Garthe disguise could get him close enough to the monster truck to plant inside the wheel well. Goliath without wheels was no threat to anything. The detonator box of the concussion cap nestled just below the vital signs monitor. Michael stifled a surge of admiration for the wonderful job April had done on such short notice.

'What about this car?' Rita said. 'Won't it look suspicious, you rolling up in Michael Knight's car, claiming to be Garthe?'

'I thought about that, too,' said Michael. 'If Garthe had sought me out, and defeated me, what better proof to trot in front of Elizabeth Bishop and Tsombe Kuna than my own car – the car that Knight Industries gave to Michael Knight, instead of to Garthe? His ego would demand a display like that.'

Rita mulled that over for a minute. 'You know, you're absolutely right. He'd brag about it. Personal accomplishment means everything to him.'

'Michael, I'm picking up heavy equipment readings,' said KITT.

'Lay 'em on me, old buddy.'

'A large trailer or recreational vehicle. Several jeeps or small cars. A large aircraft, engines off, parked some hundred yards or so from the vehicle cluster. And... Michael! It's there!'

'What?'

'Goliath is present. I'm picking up the peculiar spiky configurations on my waveform monitor that can only indicate the presence of the Bonded Molecular Shell. The dimensions correlate to those of Goliath!'

'Michael,' Rita said, suddenly nervous. 'I think Garthe planned to kill me as well as Ron. He'd used me up. What if he told Elizabeth, or Kuna? Wouldn't it look suspicious for Garthe to show up in Rita's company all of a sudden?'

'I can think up some Garthe-like excuse,' he said as he increased speed. The desert hardpan raced past the windows, gradually giving way to the parched salt flat that designated the outer limits of Dry Lake. He saw the brightly-coloured canvas of Tsombe Kuna's rainbow sunshade first of all. 'No, better yet, just stay in the car. There's nothing they can do to you as long as you're inside. KITT can darken the windows so they won't even see you – just lay low.'

He decided not to mention that trusting in KITT's protection against the onslaught of Goliath was what had almost netted him a broken back, and had rendered his left arm to stiff, painful uselessness. He was steering KITT one-handed. After smashing his plaster cast on Garthe's exceptionally hard head, Michael had demurred getting a replacement. Wearing the cast would have made his impersonation of Garthe impossible, so he went without it . . . keeping the pain to himself.

They could see Goliath now, chrome winking at them in the sunlight, totally unscathed from his encounter with KITT. A commando in a Red Beret jumped down from the truck cab and hustled over to the RV. Two other sentries had noted KITT's approach, and stood with their weapons at the ready.

There was a flutter of bright colour as Tsombe Kuna stepped from the RV. Red Berets immediately surrounded him, to protect him against the possible threat of the unidentified black street machine.

'I'm going to pull around so I can exit the car with my door away from them,' said Michael. 'With the opaqued windows, they won't have any chance of spotting you that way.'

She nodded, trusting him. 'Don't get yourself in deeper than you have to,' she said.

'Hey, you're talking to Garthe Bishop, remember? I fear no mortal.'

The Berets brought their guns up. One walked forward, signalling for Michael to come to a halt.

'Here we go,' he said, and slowed. 'KITT, monitor and record everything via comlink and your scanners. I may ask you to detonate the concussion cap via remote control. I may also ask you to get Rita out of range of Goliath if something should go wrong.'

'Just give the word, Michael,' said the car. *'Anything that puts that retarded rig out of business I'm fully prepared to*

execute.'

'Just grand.'

'Good luck, Michael,' Rita said, leaning over for a quick kiss.

'Yeah,' he said, opening the door and getting out quickly. The Red Berets were shouting in African dialect, something he was hoping he would not be called upon to fake.

At the sight of his face, they lowered their machine guns. Apparently recognition value was enough. With the moustache, his resemblance to Garthe was uncanny. The acid test for that, of course, was obvious – could he fool Garthe's own mother?

As if on cue, Elizabeth Bishop stepped down from the aluminium staircase depending from the RV. She moved grandly across the desert towards him, like a reigning queen.

'Good of you to remember our little get-together today,' she said with a hint of sarcasm. 'We thought you'd got wrapped up in a movie on cable tv, or something.'

'You don't think I'd miss my "greatest moment," do you?' he said, echoing unknowingly the words Garthe had spoken to Rita earlier.

As Michael passed, Elizabeth leaned closer and said, 'Our friend the great, world-moving revolutionary was beginning to get the quakes.'

Tsombe Kuna was staring past them at the black form of KITT. A light desert breeze stirred his ceremonial robes. 'I trust all your . . . personal vendettas have been satisfied, my brother?'

'My brother,' Michael nodded, 'you should know me better than to think I would let any vendetta, personal or otherwise, to interfere with our own personal business.' He hoped he had Garthe's tone of imperiousness down right; everyone present seemed to be eating it up. 'That thing over there is the famous Knight Industries Two Thousand. I think I shall have it compacted into a squashed cube of metal, and keep it as a coffee table curio, a memento of Michael Knight's defeat.'

Tsombe shrugged; this whole line of conversation had become, for him, nonproductive. He was anxious to get on with the Red Bluff raid. Beyond them, near Goliath, a group of Red Berets with backpacks, gas masks and weapons began to assemble.

'I assume everything is in readiness,' Michael said. Beneath his silk shirt, the cool metal of the concussion cap pressed into the flesh of his stomach. If the compact little bomb were to go off right now, the whole PALM movement would be crushed . . . but there wouldn't be enough left of Michael to spread on a cracker.

'As you can see, my commandos are awaiting orders,' said Tsombe proudly.

'Excellent. I need five minutes to run a prelim check on Goliath.' He turned and headed for the big black truck, flourishing his cane as he walked.

Elizabeth returned to the RV, but Tsombe lingered. 'My brother Garthe,' he called out, intercepting Michael halfway to the truck.

'Yes?'

'Is there something wrong with your arm?' Tsombe pointed at the one opposite the hand holding the diamond-headed cane.

'No. I'm fine.' To prove it, Michael flexed both arms. White-hot agony slammed up his left arm and set his brain on fire; it felt as though a molten rivet had just been plugged into the soft flesh opposite his elbow. The bloody arm was broken, all right, and grinding itself away like a gear full of sand.

'I only thought that perhaps if you were injured, one of my drivers could –'

'No! Only I deal with Goliath for this mission, Tsombe, haven't I made that clear by now?'

All heads turned at the sound of a furious honking. At first Michael thought KITT was attempting some kind of diversionary ploy. While everyone's attention was mis-directed, he was able to key the comlink.

'KITT? What is it?'

'Michael, a car is approaching at high speed from the south. You can hear the horn. I don't recognize the vehicle.'

He considered running for the truck, to plant the concussion cap. He was still too far away not to look conspicuous.

See if you can get a video image, KITT, and tell me what you see.'

After a moment of silence, KITT reported dolefully, *'Michael, I think it's Garthe Bishop.'* Then he added, *'The real one, I mean.'*

14

When Garthe awoke, hot blue sputtering light blinded him.

His eyes focused and he found himself staring at a twin row of fluorescent light tubes. *Two*, he thought, *two just alike . . .*

Then his head filled up with Michael Knight, and he came fully back to consciousness in a rage.

Head throbbing, a blue welt beneath the hair covering the occipital ridge of his skull – a souvenir from the hood lip of his own Corvette – he sat up on the camp bed. His vision swam and jags of residual pain slipped through his head like blades of glass. He'd been walloped a good one all right.

The room was a windowless 10 x 10 box with the camp bed, a kitchen chair, a low table, an ottoman and an institutional steel desk shoved into one corner. Everything was mismatched; it seemed to be a room with no purpose other than odd storage; it clearly wasn't designed as a storeroom.

Garthe checked for air or heating vents that might be used for escape; there were none except for a useless grille about the size of a paperback book just above the door. There was no transom he could shimmy through.

Perfunctorily, he twisted the doorknob. Locked – and not a flimsy privacy lock, either.

Instead of letting his anger take over, he circled the room several times, almost pacing. What he was doing was adjusting his mind to consider this obstacle to his progress; it was a mystic discipline he had come by during his long hours in the rat-infested Tongo M'Kimbe dungeons. Faceless soldiers had thrown him their garbage, and he and Tsombe had eaten it, during that purgatory of imprisonment. What little water they had been given had tasted like it had been used to wax the floor of a varnish factory. The food – if it could be termed that – was always dregs and lees. Never enough. Garthe had eaten spiders to supplement his diet, down there in the dark. They'd tried to break him with starvation, with isolation, with beatings without number. Once, the torture crew had tied him down, then tied a fat, ugly Rhinoceros viper near his face. The hideous, triangular serpent – with one of the most potent venoms in the world – had been just about to shed its skin, and was blinded; the isinglass-thin membranes covering its eyes had clouded up preparatory to the shedding of the old skin. Unable to see, it struck blindly at anything with body heat. It struck at Garthe, repeatedly, its fangs slashing the air an inch short of his face each time. The viper could not see, but Garthe could, and he would not give his captors the pleasure of screaming despite the very real possibility that the rope holding the snake might slip that one crucial inch, or it might break free with its thick body, to spike him. It had gone on for hours, in a hot, black room lit only by candles and stinking of sweat and decay.

Garthe had no way of knowing it, but the experience had been another link tying his destiny to that of Michael Knight, who had endured similar trials while roped to poles of bamboo in a Viet Cong prison camp during the Indochina war.

He drank in the image of his new prison. It was clean, pristine, with white walls and the hum of conditioned air. It flickered, and before his eyes became the night-hole, the pit in which he'd suffered in Africa. And all his well-honed survival mechanisms locked smoothly in and began whirring inside his head.

There were no video cameras he could perceive monitoring the room, but there might have been microphones. That was fine; he did not need to talk to himself as he worked.

He was still wearing the dinner jacket ensemble he had on for the showdown at the crap table at the MGM Grand. The tie hung loosely, like a dead carnation. He still had his belt on.

He dragged the kitchen chair to the centre of the room, and eyed the steel plumbing pipes intersecting on the ceiling. Yes, he thought. The pipes meant he was probably on a lower floor, perhaps even on ground level. A hole in the ground, like the torture pit at the Tongo M'Kimbe death camp.

Garthe had learned to endure some pretty interesting types of pain in that camp. How to cease breathing. How to meditate away the pain of a broken jaw. How to feed off his own body when there was nothing to eat, not even the blind white grubs he sometimes dug out of the dirt walls.

He unlooped the dress belt from around his waist, moved under the intersection of plumbing pipes, and smiled to himself.

They had no idea what he was capable of.

'I'm worried about Michael's arm,' April said, two floors above the room where Garthe had been locked up for the morning.

'What exactly did the doctor tell you?' said Devon. He moved across the room to his desk and sat down.

April was occupying her usual berth in front of the computer console. She looked slightly fatigued. 'Dr Alpert said that the tumble Michael took inside of KITT came this far from snapping his forearm in two places.' She held her thumb and forefinger a quarter of an inch apart. 'The more stress he puts on that arm, the greater the likelihood he'll complete the hairline fractures and complicate them. Just giving up on the sling doubles his chances of messing himself up. He nearly rendered his arm totally useless when he broke the cast over Garthe's head last night. His left shoulder socket is in bad shape – he almost dislocated it when KITT was wrecked. He reported a little blurred vision. He might have a concussion we don't know about. He might blackout while he's planting the bomb on Goliath . . .' Her voice suddenly caught in her throat.

Devon diplomatically turned his attention away from her obvious grief. 'You've gotten pretty complete information,' he said quietly.

'Like I said, I'm worried.' Then she made a fist and firmed

up. 'No, Devon, damn it, it isn't right. He runs out there like some character in a spy novel, and every mission he conks his head or wrenches his tendons. You know how, in novels, the hero sometimes gets knocked out three or four times per book? You know what happens when you hit someone hard enough to render them unconscious –?'

'I've had some experience with the sensation, yes,' said Devon.

'Sometimes you screw up nerves, sometimes you burst a lot of capillaries just below the surface of the skin. Internal bleeding, Devon. Pinprick haemorrhages. Little bunches of neurons in the brain cease to exist, the way the brain cells of an alcoholic die a few more with every drink. Then one day you keel over, bingo, because you've developed a haematoma, or your brain is drowning in unoxygenated blood, or you suddenly go blind or can't keep your balance any more, and all because . . .'

'April, you're upsetting yourself.'

She pressed on. '*All because* some stubborn idiots think life is a comic book or a John Wayne movie where nobody ever gets hurt for real!'

'What's your point?' he said clinically, wondering where she was headed with this passionate lecture.

'What right do we have to make him go out there and get himself killed for us?' She seemed to peter out, to lose energy. 'I guess that's it.'

'Michael is and always has been a volunteer.'

She knew him too well for him to get away with that claim. 'Yeah, just the way you and I are volunteers, right? Face it, Devon, we get a big kick out of playing the good guys with the white hats – and that's fine when you're living in a comic book, I guess. People never die from blood clots in the comics.'

'Michael considered the risk worth hurting his arm. He doesn't *enjoy* pain, you know.'

'I know,' she said. 'And this time it's just his arm. But what about next time? How many times has he been in the hospital already? In an ambulance? Think hard. And when you're done, think about this: how many *more* times does he have before he starts falling down without warning, before the fluid imbalance in his inner ear, say, causes him to start walking into doorjambs, *wham*!'

'Michael's an adventurer,' said Devon. 'We couldn't stop him taking risks even if we wanted to. I think he's come to enjoy danger. He mentioned something along those lines the other day. He said that even *he* didn't know if he had a choice whether or not to always tread the path of safety and convenience. Adventurers love danger, it's true. And I think Michael does.'

'Marvellous.'

'He makes it worse, because of his position. Just think: if *you* had KITT, and the resources of Knight Industries at your beck and call, plus unlimited finances and informational access . . . what kind of extreme risks might you wind up considering, merely to entertain yourself? Most of the people in the world are concerned with the struggle for fiscal survival. It's been my observation that with that struggle removed, the breadwinner, with no primary motivation left, moves to risk to regain the struggle.'

'You mean, like, a hardworking guy suddenly wins the Irish Sweepstakes?'

'Yes – he doesn't have to do the job he thinks he hates, anymore. He gets bored with spending money sooner than he would've thought possible. He turns to artificial stimulants to replace the endless Sisyphus-like struggle that used to be the core of his life. Alcohol, drug addiction. Or he takes up hang-gliding, mountain climbing, parachuting – you'll notice how many of these pastimes cost a substantial ground-floor investment of money. Our theoretical breadwinner puts excitement back in his life by putting his life in danger, since at that point it's literally the only thing he's got left to lose. Or he spends the rest of his days sitting in front of a video screen. Everything is piped in; he doesn't have to do a thing but sit in his chair and eat – it's the most utterly safe activity there is.

But it's not living.'

'You mean Michael proves he's alive by risking his life constantly?' And in this case, she added mentally, risking his limb as well.

'Yes. A very smart fellow named de Lhandes once pointed out that most people equate death with violence when, in fact, violence is the opposite of death, since violence is generally concerned with the struggle to live. The violence that results from a mugging –'

'Is the fight to keep from dying,' April said. 'So Michael denies death through his addiction to danger.'

'But that addiction is like deficit-financing. If you indulge it too much, you'll hasten the very thing you're trying, at all cost, to avoid. And that's where we must work on Michael psychologically. He is not, as you have noticed, the most emotionally stable person in FLAG.'

'He *is* cute, though,' she said, and Devon frowned. 'Speaking of life and death, I suppose it's time to make sure our prisoner didn't shuffle off this mortal coil during the night . . . ?'

'Yes – though it certainly would have simplified everything if Garthe had died in Africa. I'll go.' With the air of a man who despises the task at hand, Devon opened his desk drawer and withdrew a small gun, a nickel-plated .32 calibre Italian automatic, a souvenir of some earlier mission.

He hated using guns. It ran against his whole philosophy that firepower was not the way to solve the problems of the modern world. Firepower, the bigger stick, had been used since the dawn of time, and humankind still had not got the idea that it didn't work. Wilton Knight had been devoted to that idea as well – it was one of the reasons KITT did not feature offensive weaponry like front-mounted machine guns.

Devon took the lift down to the basement and dug out the keys for the storage room door. He worked the action on the little gun to make sure the clip was loaded, then he inserted the key.

The room was utterly quiet inside.

'Stand back from the door,' he announced for Garthe's benefit. 'I am armed.'

He waited a second, then swung the door back.

Garthe Bishop hung from the plumbing pipes, his dress belt buckled around his neck, sinking deeply into the flesh there. His eyes had rolled ceilingward in his skull and his tongue protruded darkly. His feet, toed-in and hanging in the air three feet above the floor, swayed with the air compression caused by the opening door. He appeared to have been dead for half the night.

Adrenalin rushed through him, and he took a step into the room. 'April!' he shouted down the corridor.

Garthe's eyes snapped open, insanely white. He grabbed the belt above his head and arched, kicking Devon in the face with his shining dress shoes.

Devon's arms windmilled and he fell backward, crashing over the desk in the corner. The Italian automatic went off with a nasty *spatting* sound, and a round drilled a neat dime-sized hole in the panelling.

Garthe yanked his special slipknot free and dropped to the floor. Before Devon could bring the gun up again the younger man caught his head between his open palms, slap-slapping it back and forth. Devon's head rebounded limply, like the bulb on a dead flower, and he blacked out.

Garthe snatched up the gun just as April came out of the lift at a dead run.

Garthe sprang to a position just behind the door, and when April stuck her head in he palmed the pistol and struck her full in the face with it, shattering her cheekbone.

He wanted to save the bullets for Michael Knight.

April went down as though she'd been hit with a ball-peen hammer.

Leaving his belt dangling from the sewage pipe, its golden buckle glittering, he lifted Devon's limp wrist to check the time. The deadline for commencement of the Red Bluff operation was imminent.

On the floor, April's pulverized cheek began to drain to an ominous violet colour. Garthe stepped over her body on the way out the door.

Upstairs he found the keys to Devon's collector's item Bentley, and made his escape in minutes.

15

At first, Michael thought he was hallucinating. He saw Devon's vintage Bentley, the one with the heavy-duty supercharger, tearing across the desert hardpan at top speed, and for a vertiginous moment thought that his FLAG superior had some emergency reason for showing up in person, to blow his cover as 'Garthe.'

Then he spotted the madman at the wheel, and knew the jig was up. KITT had been right – it was Garthe, against all odds that could be computed.

Tsombe Kuna was waving his arms and shouting.

Michael made his decision, and turned and ran for Goliath.

The Red Berets milling around the truck box turned their attention towards him. They could not yet hear what Kuna was yelling.

The Bentley roared through the RV encampment, clipping one of the picnic poles, causing the rainbow tarpaulin to sag to the ground. Dust plumed up from the rear wheels as Garthe's maniac driving abused the transmission.

The Berets could now see that Garthe and Michael looked exactly the same. Michael was still thirty yards from the truck. When he glanced back over his shoulder he saw the grille of the Bentley, and as Garthe tried to mow him down with the car, Michael was forced to dive onto his injured arm, snapping his forearm like a chopstick. He rolled in the dirt and tried to get to his feet again. KITT was calling for him over the comlink, but Michael couldn't hear it above the sudden pounding of blood in his ears.

Garthe stomped on the Bentley's brakes, nearly totalling the car against Goliath's alloyed flank, and jumped from the seat doing the one thing that would firmly establish his true identity to the Red Berets – he shouted orders in the African dialect he and Tsombe Kuna often spoke to each other.

The soldiers responded, running to Michael, machine guns levelled at him. The concussion cap lay in the dust five feet from his broken arm.

A second later, Michael looked up . . . and into the bore of the Italian automatic from Devon's desk.

'So we meet again, my "brother,"' Garthe said sarcastically.

A pair of commandos wrestled Michael to his feet. He gasped as his broken arm was wrenched in a new and unpleasant direction.

Tsombe Kuna and Elizabeth caught up with the group. 'Garthe!' his mother shouted. 'What's the meaning of all this?'

'So sorry I'm late, Mother, dear,' Garthe returned with effected calm. 'I had a little *doppelganger* problem to clear up. But it's all better now.'

He shoved the pistol into the hollow of Michael's throat, and for a heart-jumping second everyone present thought they were going to get sprayed with Michael Knight's departing brains. But instead, Garthe reached forward and peeled the phony moustache from Michael's face, like a general stripping a turncoat of his military decorations and brass buttons.

'I'm pleased you're here, Michael,' he said fraternally. 'I want you to witness my triumph over you, over Devon Miles, over FLAG, and over the entire country. Then perhaps I'll shoot you . . . if you're lucky.'

'It's people like you,' Michael spat, 'who give revolutions a bad name.'

'Revolution, pshaw,' Garthe said, getting a steely look from Tsombe, who hated to hear one of his favourite words abused. 'This is a *personal* conquest; surely you can appreciate that better than anyone here. You and I, we're enemies because we're so bloody alike. You have the principles, the ideas, the white hat, so to speak. I have the darker powers on my side.

You play Abel to my Cain. And since I am about to avail myself to all those things you have received in my stead, it pleases me to know that very soon, *you* shall share in the fruits I have reaped over long and bitter years.' Twenty gun muzzles stayed aimed at Michael's face as Garthe reached forward and patted his cheek. He left Michael's phony diamond glue-on earring where it was.

'What's that supposed to mean?' said Michael, grimacing through the fogbank of pain his arm was laying down before his eyes. 'Other than the fact that you are a stark, raving lunatic?' He smiled, throwing Garthe's bogus, snake-like charm back at him.

'Upon the completion of my mission here, my good friend Tsombe Kuna and I shall return to the Africa we love. You'll come with us and be our honoured guest, of course.'

About a hundred yards away, KITT sat, awaiting instructions, outwardly empty. The comlink was on Michael's broken arm, and he dared not risk trying to use it when any sudden movement would make a hailstorm of bullets vapourize his head.

'As you no doubt know from your data pulls on my history,' Garthe said, in spite of the fact Kuna was beginning to vibrate with agitation over being a moment late for the Red Bluff raid, 'Tsombe and I escaped from the Tongo M'Kimbe death camp, in the Jimbaru province. Tsombe's Red Berets liberated Jimbaru . . . but Tongo M'Kimbe still exists. The place where I suffered, while my blood father turned his back on me, and gave you my destiny on a platter.'

Michael shook his head disgustedly. 'You're crazy, Garthe. It wasn't like that at all.'

Garthe's arm lashed out, slapping Michael, whipping his head around, striating his neck muscles, causing his arm to complain even more. Blood filled the tiny spaces between Michael's teeth.

'As I said, Tongo M'Kimbe still exists. And when we all return to Africa, you shall become its only permanent resident. The Red Beret have been honing new methods of persuasion for those who oppose PALM's revolution... methods that will require testing on live subjects, to gauge their efficacy.' He leaned closer, his nose an inch away from Michael's. 'It shall please me very much to watch you scream, and beg for your life, as I take my face off of your body, a strip of flesh at a time. The process has been known to take weeks. And then we'll feed you to the soldier ants.'

Michael stayed calm, unruffled. 'There's nothing you can do to me, Garthe. You can't even keep my attention for very long. You're dull-witted and deluded... and tomorrow morning, you're going to wake up in a padded closet.'

Whack! Another slap. Michael tasted blood, but the taste of Garthe slowly losing control, bordering on paranoiac hysteria, was smoother.

'Let's go to it, Tsombe. You man the plane; I'll man Goliath.' He barked brief orders to the Red Berets, and Michael found himself shouldered up between two of them, who dogtrotted him back to the waiting Winnebago.

'It is time at last,' Tsombe grinned broadly.

'Yes, my brother. We have, as I believe some historical figure said, our rendezvous with destiny.'

Inside the RV was a huge video-beam setup, designed to give Elizabeth, Tsombe, Kumenya and the soldiers a first-hand view of the action as it occurred. Goliath, among other things, featured alloy-shielded video cameras on swivel mounts, electronically controlled.

'Just like Monday night football,' said Michael.

'Have a seat, Michael,' said Elizabeth, as though she was hostessing a cocktail party. 'A ringside seat for a historic moment.'

'Not to mention a moment that will make several people's bank accounts quite healthy,' said Michael.

'Wealth,' Tsombe laughed, 'is the curse of the privileged. Loyalty is worth millions. I have both – my diamond mines, my Red Berets.' He seemed to be playing the benevolent *poohah*, the big chief, for everyone present.

Michael wondered what Devon and April were doing, and how Garthe could have escaped the Foundation office . . . and how he could contact KITT without attracting attention in the confines of the RV. He knew KITT was listening to every word, via the comlink . . . but without orders the car would do nothing on its own initiative.

In the distance, Garthe slipped of his tuxedo – what remained of it – and snaked into a skintight black jump-suit laden with silver zippers, his combat uniform for the afternoon. Just the chic item for a diverting little raid on a government missile dump. In full view of the camera, he climbed into Goliath's cab and fired up the monster diesel powerhouse.

'Egomaniac,' Michael muttered. Most of the watchers ignored his jibe. Good – that was just what he wanted.

Goliath's triple rack of airhorns emitted a bone-shaking victory blast that pealed throughout the valley beyond the salt flats. Then the gigantic machine began to roll. The last few commandos in the cluster of Red Berets jumped onto the rear of the truck while it was moving away, and closed the massive doors.

'Just like the Trojan Horse,' said Elizabeth. The reference was lost on Tsombe, who was thinking of the African child's fable of the Elephant and the Monkey.

An Elephant hated the insistent chattering of the Monkey. The Monkey chattered so because he was hungry, and could not reach the fruit on the trees, which were slippery with recent rains, and impossible to climb. Often the Elephant tried to step on the Monkey and stop his noise for good. One day, while the Elephant was asleep, the Monkey clambered onto his back, which was not slippery. When the Elephant awoke, he was unaware of the Monkey's presence. When the Elephant stood up, the Monkey could reach the fruit. The Monkey ate heartily, while the Elephant wondered what had happened to the hungry, chattering little beast. Finally, the Monkey could keep the joke to himself no longer, and jumped down, laden with fruit, which he shared with the Elephant. They became friends, and agreed to work their food-gathering system every day. After their first hearty meal, they found a place to sleep – the Elephant on the ground, the Monkey by the Elephant's side. But the Elephant always snored after a full meal, and this kept the Monkey awake. The Monkey punched his new friend on the side to quiet him down, whereupon the Elephant, stuffed with food and dreaming, rolled over in his sleep and crushed the Monkey into the earth. The next morning, the Elephant awoke and could not find his new friend . . . but was happy, at least, that the Monkey was not starving. Eventually he came to miss even the noisy chattering.

Tsombe saw himself as the all-powerful Elephant, and Garthe as the foolish Monkey . . . and it would be payoff time soon enough.

Michael did not know that fable, but he knew about the Trojan Horse, mentioning, 'Even Troy fell, and those who crushed Troy with their wooden horse were themselves defeated.'

'Perhaps,' she said, uncaring. 'As long as we're not defeated in *my* lifetime.'

Red Bluff was coming up on the video monitor. Goliath was rolling towards the restriction fence at top speed. Michael could read the lettering on the sign he'd first seen a few days before –

RESTRICTED GOVERNMENT LAND. ADMINISTERED BY BUREAU OF INDIAN AFFAIRS. KEEP OUT. TRESPASSERS WILL BE PROSECUTED.

What a joke, he thought.

The screen went white momentarily as Goliath burst through the fence, smashing the sign to pieces and bearing down directly on the huge double doors of lead, set into the mountainside, in the dim distance.

'A marvellous plan, with an elegant *denouement*,' Kuna was saying. 'Goliath also features three hundred and sixty degrees of nozzles. You'll see the system in action very shortly.'

'Gas?' said Michael, catching on. 'Of course. Gas for the

guards inside the missile dump.'

'If the gods are with us, we shall not have to fire a single shot to be victorious.'

'What are you using, Kuna?'

Tsombe smiled, not unlike Garthe's evil grin. 'Delta Nine.'

'Then it doesn't matter if you shoot the guards or not, does it?' he said. 'Delta Nine is nerve gas, and fatal. Our own government killed a lot of bighorn sheep with it by accident a few years ago. Now even crabgrass won't grow on the site.'

'It matters not,' said Kuna. 'Soldiers – all soldiers – are aware of the fortunes of war. And as for things growing ... who cares? Who cares what grows in the middle of a desert, or a salt flat wasteland like this, eh?'

It became clear to Michael that Tsombe Kuna was at least as insane as Garthe Bishop.

Goliath hit the blast doors head-on, with a sound like a cinderblock dropped into an oil drum. Then it backed up. The huge doors had buckled radically. One more strike from the impervious truck would burst them. Alarms were going off crazily and danger lights were flashing.

Garthe charged the blast doors a second time, and they fell with double clangs. When the dust cleared, Michael could see soldiers in desert fatigues running out with automatic weapons and peppering Goliath with rounds. The bullets skimmed off the Bonded Molecular Shell like grains of salt.

And then the soldier nearest to Goliath's cab clutched his throat, dropped his weapon in mid-burst, and collapsed limply to the floor, where he lay twitching.

'Delta Nine is colourless and odourless,' Tsombe said. 'An elegant denouement, as I have said.'

'Mass murder,' said Michael. 'If only Maddux hadn't been such a jackass ...'

'Watch it,' said Elizabeth. 'You're talking about the man I love. At least, *he* thinks so.' She smiled enigmatically.

Michael felt like an utter sap. So *that* was why General Maddux had been so unco-operative! Elizabeth had got to him first ... just as he had got to Kyle Elliot down in Rio de

Janiero.

Red Berets wearing full-face gas masks began to come into camera view, mopping up quickly. In less than sixty seconds, Garthe and his force had overrun Red Bluff and rendered its defences useless. It was a meticulously planned, flawless raid, pulled off with precision timing. Garthe Bishop sure didn't kid around...

Tsombe Kuna was watching the giant video screen like a sports fan, wildly enthusiastic. Elizabeth, vaguely bored that her part in the operation was done, moved to the kitchen of the RV to freshen up her drink. Michael glanced at the guards on either side of him, and realized it was now or never.

Over the commotion onscreen, which even had most of the attention of the Red Berets still inside the Winnebago, Michael raised his unresponsive and pulsing arm. Swelling had commenced, bloating his forearm so that the comlink was cutting off his circulation.

'Set off the cap and ram us,' he said simply. 'Now.'

The guards looked at him strangely, and for a moment, he thought KITT had not registered his request.

Then, outside, the lost concussion cap detonated with a report that vibrated the RV, digging a huge crater into the ground.

'What the hell was that?' cried Elizabeth, so startled that she dropped her drink on the counter.

Tsombe barked orders to his men, and three of the Red Berets made for the RV's door...

... just as KITT, fullspeed, rammed the opposite side of the Winnebago. The top-heavy mobile home rocked radically on its springs, and dumped the foremost Red Beret out the screen door through sheer momentum.

Down the short hallway, Michael saw KITT's gleaming black prow destroy the bathroom. The toilet became a projectile that tore through the far wall, obliterating the video beam screen. Tsombe Kuna screamed and ducked, shielding his head. The Red Berets leaped to aid their fallen master.

And Michael jumped up, planting his elbow in the nearest

Red Beret's mouth. The man fell backward and Michael galloped down the short hall. In one jump, his feet landed on KITT's hood.

He slipped and fell onto his wounded arm again, a cry of pain escaping him. Elizabeth had already picked up one of the Red Beret's machine guns and was just coming into view where the door for the RV's bathroom had once been.

'Go, go, *go*!' he screamed as the pilot-side door popped open, and he scrambled towards it.

Elizabeth laid down two neat bursts right across KITT's windscreen. Michael had to slam the door with his right arm, reaching clumsily across. The slugs skipped off the alloyed glass, leaving spark trails like tiny meteorites, and Rita hit the deck with a yelp, certain her head was being shot off.

'Nudge her, KITT, and let's go get Goliath!'

KITT's rear wheels dug out, and the black car withdrew from the punctured side of the RV. Then the car lurched forward, knocking the rocking Winnebago, and Elizabeth Bishop lost her balance, falling backwards onto her rich and privileged rump, firing as she fell, bullets stitching the ceiling panels of the RV.

Rita laughed as she witnessed Elizabeth's inglorious fall.

'How's the charge on the resonating laser, old buddy?' Michael said.

'Full. But Michael, the vital signs monitor indicates your arm is broken, and in vital need of medical attention. We'll have to –'

'No time, KITT! We've got to stop Goliath from making its rendezvous with that plane on time! Now shut up and give me full speed to Red Bluff!'

Lights scampered about on the Super Dash and the AUTO PURSUIT mode engaged. Then they were travelling at fifty, then a hundred miles per hour.

'Goliath is on our heading already, Michael,' reported KITT. *'Sonic scan reveals that the box contains a cluster of the SHOR-ATTAC missiles.'*

'Damn! Garthe must have had a ramp set up inside the truck box! I was hoping to catch him still inside the cave, where Goliath couldn't be manoeuvred!'

'You mean we're going to have to take him on out in the open, with nothing but a resonating laser?' said KITT obviously dismayed. *'Michael, we'll get turned into scrap again. I can't handle getting destroyed twice in one week. There's something else, too.'*

'Yeah?'

'I'm picking up the Knight Industries semi approaching from the southwest, across the salt flat. No transmissions as yet.'

'Keep it that way,' responded Michael. 'I don't want to argue with Devon while our hands are full with Goliath.'

To his right, blueprints on Goliath danced across one of the monitor screens faster than his eyes could follow. KITT was gulping down information, searching for a potential weak spot – *any* weak spot that could be used against Garthe.

'There he is,' said Rita, pointing.

Michael looked up and saw Goliath charging at them across the expanse of desert floor. The brain-rattling airhorn went off once, twice, like a call to combat.

'Michael, you're not thinking of charging him head-on again, are you?'

'This time we modify the plan,' he said, flooring the accelerator. 'Ever see a bullfight, KITT?'

'Barbaric entertainment.'

'Good. Because you and I are going to play the red rag, and try to fake out the bull. Goliath's got the size, but we've got the speed. Give us the harnesses.'

The shoulder straps dropped down automatically for Michael and Rita. She had to help him into his because of his useless arm. 'Is this going to . . . uh, hurt?' she asked, fear in her eyes.

'Just a little high speed manoeuvring,' Michael assured her. 'No sweat.' There was literally no sweat on his forehead; his complexion had gone completely white. He had to get to a doctor soon, or pass out. 'Tell me, KITT, can we cut the trailer loose from the tractor if we hit the hitch dead on with a shot from the laser?'

'Possibly. My scan reveals a potential unalloyed component in the trailer hitch.'

'We'll make that our first target. Don't let him fake us out again, like he did last time. Leave yourself plenty of room to dodge. The truck is more cumbersome despite its speed. And if we can cut the trailer loose, it'll be as top-heavy as that Winnebago. Maybe we can tip Goliath over. But first, flash past him, then do a high speed turn and come at him from a tight angle, so we have a clear shot at the hitch.'

'Wish me luck, Michael . . .'

Then Goliath was on top of them.

The monster truck was travelling much faster than Michael had expected, and KITT's rear wheels locked as the brakes took them into a sideways skid. Their rear bumper missed Goliath's killer grille by inches, and a dense cloud of brown smoke rolled up, partially obscuring them from view.

'Now!' Michael yelled. 'Get right behind him and floor it!'

KITT rapidly caught up with the rear end of the trailer box.

'Now, buddy, fuse the latch on that thing so the commandos and the SHOR-ATTACs are sealed in. And make sure you don't penetrate the door and set off one of those nukes . . . or we'll all be radioactive dust over Utah!'

The Super Dash recorded the power drain as the laser fired, on target. Hitting the hitch on the moving truck would be harder.

Michael had a sudden flash of inspiration. 'KITT – Goliath, except for the Bonded Molecular Shell, is just an ordinary truck, right? Just an exceptionally large, reinforced, ordinary truck?'

'Of course, Michael. Why?'

It hit him like a thunderbolt. Goliath had no computers, no microprocessors, no offensive weaponry (other than the gas jets, which need not concern KITT). No contingencies for the sorts of things KITT was equipped to handle every day. If Goliath was crippled, no ramjet unit would automatically drop from the equipment bay. It would just sit there. Except for the armoured skin, like KITT's, and the puncture-proof tyres, like KITT's . . . Goliath was nothing more than a normal big rig, the kind you see hauling vegetables to the Safeway market.

'Speed up on the outside,' he said. 'Let's take a shot at that trailer hitch.'

The red digits on the speedometer jumped from 100 to 135 mph.

Garthe saw them coming in the big outboard mirrors, and swerved to sideswipe them. KITT ducked nimbly out of the way. The truck could not make knife-sharp turns at high speed; it would tip over like an elephant with a slit throat. KITT bobbed and weaved. One monitor continued to blur through Goliath's schematics, the other computed the most probable pathway that would open up the space between the truck tractor and the trailer for a shot. All KITT would need, once locked in, was about a quarter of a second.

Suddenly a dotted-line course on the monitor lit up in neon green. It was a wide, looping trajectory that called for them to shoot ahead of the truck, then bore in from the starboard side, a course that accounted for Garthe's fastest evasive-driving reaction. It was perfect. There was no time for argument.

'Implementing,' said KITT, and their speed jumped again.

'Hang on, Rita!'

KITT applied his TURBO BOOST function to leap several car lengths ahead, then cut across Goliath's path. There was a heart-wrenching moment when they were directly in front of the truck, Michael's side-to, and Garthe laid on the airhorn again, when it looked like they were going to be obliterated, but magically they slid into a speed turn on the opposite side.

The board lit up again as the laser fired.

There was a sparking orange corona of impact on the trailer hitch, then the box disengaged, slipping away from Goliath's cab at well over sixty miles per hour.

'Hang onto his tail!' Don't let him get us head-on again!'

KITT complied. *'Aren't you going to compliment me on my*

aim?'

'Just great,' said Rita. 'But Goliath and Garthe are still in the race, so no applause just yet, huh?'

Garthe slammed on his hydraulic brakes, decelerating, and KITT rammed the truck from behind, crumpling his recently replaced alloy prow.

'Ouch!'

'Come on,' Michael chided. 'Back off. Nothing's hurt but your pride.' *'I'm afraid it's a bit more than that, Michael. The power pack on the resonating laser is bleeding energy. If we don't fire within the next fifteen seconds, we won't be able to fire.'*

'Holy –!' Michael stood on the brakes and twisted the wheel with his good arm. Goliath had skidded around broadside right in front of them and the two vehicles now faced each other. KITT slid to a dusty halt inches from Goliath's grille.

For a horrible second, they were looking up into Garthe's laughing face, looming above them, mouth wide with sadistic glee as he tooted his airhorn.

'Back off! Back off!' Michael shouted. 'Get some distance! Try to get a shot at his axle!'

KITT dug out, hauling backwards at a good seventy. *'Ten seconds, Michael,'* he announced.

The airhorn was still blatting mightily.

'When he accelerates, the front of the cab should come off the ground just enough for me to sneak a shot in,' KITT said. *'But we've only got five seconds to do it.'*

'He'll sit there and wait, unless we make him charge,' said Michael. 'Let's do it!'

He floored the accelerator again and charged Goliath, head-on, the one thing he'd hoped to avoid.

The airhorn quit as Garthe geared up and engaged speed.

'Shoot through the windshield!' said Michael. 'Try to start a fire in the cab!'

'Two seconds,' reported KITT.

'He's moving!' shouted Rita. 'Fire, fire!'

KITT cut loose his first burst as the chromed steel of the crash bumper rose barely perceptible inches with Garthe's acceleration. The beam spanged off the underside of the bumper and chewed halfway through the heavy duty axle. Goliath was still rolling towards them, gaining speed, coming at them like a bad guy in a tv western, from the dead opposite side of the valley.

KITT tried to fire a second shot just as the power pack died. Michael saw a crimson reflection bounce from the cab windshield with no visible results.

'Sorry, Michael.'

'Never mind about that!' There was no more distance left between the two juggernauts. 'Evasive turbo boost, now!'

With the characteristic *whoosh* of air compression, KITT took to the sky at a forty-five degree angle, wheels clipping the top of Goliath's cab as they went whizzing overhead.

Rita screamed, not knowing what to expect.

They landed hard, jogging about in their seats like puppets. Michael felt something else in his arm snap like a celery stalk. A *stale* celery stalk.

'God, I can't take much more of thi –'

'Michael! Look!'

Michael cranked his head around at Rita's exclamation, fully expecting to see Goliath bearing inevitably down on them again, relentlessly. What he saw instead made his mouth drop open.

Goliath was somersaulting, going cab-over-tyres at high speed, losing parts in a multi-directional spray. Inside, Garthe was being battered about like a seed in a gourd. The two front wheels were rolling ahead of the truck, wandering away from it in a V-pattern. One of them fell over onto its side as though shot by a sniper; *plunk.* The other one spun around like a tossed coin and then settled down. Goliath was still rolling, gouging out hunks of earth with its chromed bumper, flipping onto the air, and finally coming down with a crash that burst the windows on all sides. Grey, thick smoke rolled out of the cab, and the engine of destruction was finally still.

Michael was incredulous. 'The axle must have broken . . . KITT, what happened?'

'As near as I can tell,' the machine responded, *'my shot weakened but did not destroy the axle. When Garthe saw us coming, he somehow knew that this time we were not going to try to swerve from his path, that we fully intended to meet him head-on. And he braked. The braking action at eighty-five miles per hour snapped the axle, the wheels disengaged and the cab nosed into the ground, which is what imparted the somersaulting action.'*

Michael whooped with triumph. 'He chickened out! His nerve failed him at the last minute! He braked, Rita, he braked!'

Rita could not quite believe it either.

Police units were already wailing across the salt flat towards them.

Goliath, dead, sat and smoked and was utterly still. Garthe Bishop's hand hung limply out of the cab's shattered window.

16

The group gathered in the hospital room looked like an assembly of walking wounded.

Devon strode around in the limited space, a broad swatch of tape across his nose, which had been fractured by the heel of Garthe's dress shoe. The bandage was undignified, and impeded his glasses.

April's head was wrapped in similar bandages, rather like the drummer in the famous painting of the American Revolutionaries that also featured a flag bearer and a fife player. Her bandage was more than undignified... it was unattractive. But necessary, according to Dr Alpert, since she was nursing a broken cheekbone, also courtesy of Garthe and his escape from the Foundation's Las Vegas H.Q.

Rita Wilcox seemed more or less intact. She had no idea that, at the moment, Garthe's right-hand-man and assassin, Cody Jarrett, was making tracks for the state border in his unmarked Chevy. His orders had been to kill Rita... but he had got wind of the aborted heist at Dry Lake, and much like Rita had thought earlier, had decided to save his own hide first and foremost. If she had shown up at the Flamingo suite a half-hour earlier, things might not have turned out so rosy, because Cody had only lost his nerve within that time.

They were gathered around the bed, and in the bed was Michael, his ruined left arm immobilized in a traction cast. His teeth had been loosened by Garthe's savage blow, and his voice was slightly mushy. 'Too bad you couldn't fit KITT in here, too,' he said.

'He needed more fixing up,' April said through her teeth. It obviously hurt her to move her face.

'Not just KITT,' interjected Devon. He fought to avoid

crossing his eyes over the bandage, and appearing unduly comical. 'That upstart did damage to my Bentley, as well! It needs a whole new paint job on the right-hand side!'

Wearily, Michael tried to turn his head towards Rita, then gave up. 'What happened after I passed out?'

Everyone tried to answer that one at once. After some nodding, deferrals were made.

Devon went first. 'Well, you effectively welded most of Tsombe Kuna's Red Berets into the trailer, so they and the missiles were relatively simple for the Rangers to scoop up.'

'The Rangers?'

'Called in by General Maddux himself... when he discovered that his latest girlfriend was our own Elizabeth Bishop... and that Elizabeth Bishop's paramours have the unseemly habit of sudden death.'

Michael would have shaken his head, but could not. 'Maddux. The guy who denied the missiles ever existed.'

'Oh, rest assured that the SHOR-ATTACS *don't* exist, anymore. Not on any file or record or data bank.'

'I see Maddux's Ranger force arrived just in time to save the government's neck,' muttered Michael. 'Typical military thinking...'

'At least you're alive,' said Rita.

'Elizabeth escaped in the chaos following the truck wreck,' continued Devon. 'But she showed up at Maddux's... and he turned her in. She'll serve a term for treason, at the very least.'

'Neat. Maybe Maddux deserves a pat on the back after all – it *was* Elizabeth who initiated this entire mess, not Garthe. Speaking of whom...?'

'Garthe is the only person involved in the raid who sustained more broken bones than you,' said April, a hint of happiness colouring her bruised face. 'He's in traction somewhere in the maximum-security ward, surrounded by guards, courtesy of Maddux.'

'I take this to mean no one will see dear Garthe for a long, long time?'

The agreement was unanimous, and unspoken.

'KITT destroyed Tsombe Kuna's Winnebago, so collecting him was easy,' added Devon. 'KITT had cunningly managed to impair the motorbike ramp – which was what Kuna was scampering for when the outcome of your joust with Goliath became apparent. The bike was in a compartment in the rear of the RV, and when KITT smashed through part of the wall, he bent the exit ramp for the bike. Kuna would have been overcome by carbon monoxide fumes if he'd remained in that tiny compartment much longer, revving the bike's engine. He's in custody awaiting extradition back to Africa. There is a group of people there waiting to try Kuna for much bigger crimes than the attempted theft of a few nuclear missiles.'

Dr Alpert joined the group, accompanied by a nurse. 'Time for a little injection,' he said ominously.

'Oh, great,' moaned Michael. 'Not another one.'

'I'm afraid so.'

'I have to get back to the Foundation office, my boy,' said Devon as gently as he could manage. 'There's the usual mountain of paperwork to dispense with, and this damnable bandage is already giving me a headache. You understand . . . ?'

'Sure. You have to go and do what you do best.' He squeezed the elder man's hand with his good right one.

At the threshold of the door, Devon turned and said, 'Coming, April?'

'In a moment,' she said.

'They're just waiting around to watch me get speared,' said Michael. 'Close the curtains, doc. Don't allow them this cheap thrill . . .'

Rita chuckled as the nylon drape swished into place, and they heard Michael grunting as he was rolled onto his side to receive the injection.

When Alpert re-emerged, he said, 'No physical labour for this boy for at least a month – not if he wants to keep that arm. Two months; even better. He's got a concussion I don't want to get any worse, and where the hell did he sustain so many hairline fractures? His X-rays look like splintered bark off a eucalpytus tree!'

'He falls down a lot,' said April.

When Dr Alpert stepped out, along with the nurse, Rita obligingly hung out in a nearyby waiting room for a while, so April could have a few moments alone with Michael. She told him of her fears, voiced earlier to Devon, about the scary possibility that Michael was going to drive himself right into an early grave.

Wonderingly, he said, 'You were *worried* about me?'

April nodded, her eyes moistening. 'You look pathetic in this bed, y'know? And stupid me; I got my face bashed in.'

He grasped her hand. 'You did terrific. All the things you did helped save my hide. You're more than a top-notch technician; you're a friend – above and beyond the things the Foundation, or Devon, requires you to do. So don't rag yourself. And why are you still crying?'

Her hand automatically moved to brush away tears; she had to be careful of her own bandage. 'I was just thinking . . . no lobster on Fisherman's Wharf, huh? Not for us.'

'Who told you that? Just as soon as I'm on my feet I'll –'

'No, I'm talking about Devon. He'd never allow us to go out. You're too . . . dangerous, I guess.'

'You're underestimating yourself again.' He smiled. 'You wait. You'll see, I'll pull strings. And we've got a date.'

She still had hold of his hand. 'Would you settle for some fast-food fried shrimp from Davy Jones' Locker?'

Past her injuries, he saw her as the billboard woman once again – more beautiful than ever. 'Sure thing. Provided I can chew.'

'I'll bring you something soft and mushy, okay?'

'Sounds grand.'

'Knock, knock,' said Rita from the doorway. 'The soap operas in the TV lounge are like inhaling the exhaust from a city bus. So I'm back.'

'I'm off to grab some junkfood,' said April. 'See you two in a few.' She walked through the door, careful of her stride.

'Able lady,' said Rita. 'Yours?'

'No way,' said Michael warmly. 'Not yet, at any rate. But let's talk about you.'

'Not much to talk about,' she sighed. 'I suppose Ron is avenged . . . but I don't feel any better. I miss him too much. So much for the music business . . .'

'Rita, you shouldn't give up that dream – that's the *last* thing Ron would want you to do. Let me tell you a secret –' He motioned for her to lean close so he could whisper . . . and when she did, he kissed her. The kiss lasted for a goodly time before they broke.

'Wow,' she whispered. 'Waves on the beach.'

'Always the romantic,' he reminded her, and she smiled. 'Go down to where KITT is parked. Tucked inside the Rapid Analyzer box you'll find a grubstake that I want you to take with you to Los Angeles, when you finally go.'

She stiffened. 'I'm not going *anywhere* until you do some fast healing, mister!'

'No, I mean afterward. When everything gets back to normal. There's a hundred thousand dollars stashed away in there – I want you to take it. It's the money I finessed out of Garthe in the casino.'

She cocked an eyebrow at him and he thought, *lovely, quite lovely*. 'You don't have to make that kind of offer twice, me bucko.'

'Do me a favour, then – go down, check on KITT, make sure the money's okay, and tell me how he is, hmm? If I ring him up on the comlink, he'll just lie and tell me he's miserable.' The wristwatch communicator lay in the nightstand to Michael's right.

'Sure. Back in a few.'

'KITT,' he said into the comlink, 'Rita's on her way down. How're you doing?'

'Nominal, Michael. Yourself?'

That was a good question, he thought. Lying abed, alone momentarily, he suddenly felt very mortal, and quite old. Troubleshooting for the Foundation had its myriad joys, but sometimes the trials required people with stouter bones.

What April had told him had often worried him for real . . . a worry he voiced only to KITT, and then only in partial jest. But he considered the turns his life had recently taken, and abruptly he found himself wondering: is this it? Is this all I'll do until I die? Short relationships with women who always vanish? Polite business as usual with Devon and April? No growth? Broken bones and contusions for each mission; getting guns pointed at me for the rest of my life?

No growth. That was the admission that shocked him the most. The idea that he was already performing at the peak of his capacity, that past this point in his life there was only *less* to be had.

But an endless greed for *more* was what had doomed Garthe. No, his mind corrected almost immediately; the *more* Garthe desired had always been material. The *more* Michael wanted was some higher use for his knowledge. What good was all this skill at staying alive, he thought, if all it did was keep him alive to stay alive some more?

He had to progress, using his experiences as a base for growth. It was something he intended to take up in earnest with Devon, later. Now he had time, at last, for contemplation and reflection.

He hoped he'd gain an answer from it.

'Michael? Rita has arrived,' said KITT.

Her voice came out of the tiny speaker: 'Boy, Michael, you weren't kidding about the money. It fell out in a huge pile when I opened the little black door!'

'Michael, I feel compelled to point out that the money Miss Wilcox is counting technically belongs to the Foundation. Your grubstake was secured under the heading of Foundation business – co-ordinated by Foundation equipment – and Foundation intelligence.'

'Knock it off, KITT – the grubstake I replaced. This is just between you and me and Miss Wilcox, okay?'

There was silence, then, after a moment, KITT said, 'In that event, you still owe me four hundred and thirteen dollars.'

He recalled his little computer blackjack debt. 'Uh – care to play double or nothing? I'm going to be in this bed for awhile, and –'

'Please to pay old debts before new games are begun,' KITT said humourlessly.

'KITT, I don't have a grupnik on me . . .'

'Michael,' said KITT disapprovingly, 'there are some people who would do more than break your arm for such an admission.'

'How about a loan, Michael?' came Rita's voice. 'A grubstake? I can afford it.'

Michael laughed. 'If only your old buddy Abe Plimpton could hear you say that . . .'

'Don't laugh,' she said. 'I just saw him, heading across the parking lot, in a brand spanking new leisure suit, *not* perspiring, with a blonde on one arm and a brunette on the other. I think you changed his luck, and I think he's on his way up there right now, to thank you.'

Michael rolled his eyes helplessly. Oh well, he thought, he had time. The comlink peeped beside him, and the liquid-crystal digital screen lit up with blackjack characters, blinking rapidly, going through another electronic shuffle.

'Rita's on her way back up,' said KITT. 'Shall we begin a new game?'

Michael settled back into his bed. 'Shut up and deal,' he said, grinning to himself.

ABOUT THE AUTHOR

Among ROGER HILL's varied pursuits is the calling of film historian. As he says, 'I was made the same year as John Huston's *The African Queen.*' Born in Fort Worth, Texas, and educated at the University of Iowa, Hill has worked as a journalist for major daily newspapers in Las Vegas, Seattle and Chicago. His other interests include music criticism, cartooning, photography, raising Alsatian show dogs and 'hunting for decent Thai food.' He currently resides in Studio City, California, with his wife Kendra. This is his eighth published novel.